TAKE A.I.M.

M.A. WILLIAMS

PRESS

For Jeff Hendricks

You were excited to read this book, but sadly, you were taken from this world too soon. I'll bring you a copy when I join you out there in the Universe.

CONTENTS

PROLOGUE

Dylan's heart was pounding in his chest as the A.I.M. agents closed in on his location. He'd trained for the last 6 months with Agent Larsen, but he wasn't prepared for this. He was so close to the room that his best friend, Shane, was being held in. *All that training for nothing,* he thought. *I can't die like this. Not while I'm so close.* The wound in his side was burning like hell, and the makeshift bandage was doing nothing to stop the flow of blood.

The building's loudspeaker chirped on. "We have you surrounded Dylan. Man, you were SO close. I'm here with Shane, and you're only 40 feet away. If you give up now, we won't kill you...yet. You still have a chance to live a long life if you just throw your weapons down and give up now." It was Sellers' voice.

"I'd rather die in a hail of bullets than give myself up to you! Kiss my ass Sellers!"

"That's the spirit Dylan! There's that rage I always saw in you! It won't help you anymore, but I love your enthusiasm!"

"I've already killed Kane and Mooney. Why don't you come in here and we can end this right now. Unless you're scared of a wounded teenager. Are you afraid of me Sellers?!"

He said the words, but he knew they would likely be just that: words. *I'm surrounded, bleeding profusely, and I'll most likely die from blood loss soon.* The odds didn't look good, but he had to believe that he still had a chance.

"Come on Dylan. You've got nowhere to go, you're bleeding out, and there's nothing else you can do. You tried your hardest, but it just wasn't good enough. What a bummer. I'll have everything up and running again soon, so you really haven't done anything. I'm going to give you one last chance to throw down those guns and let us take care of that wound, or you can die knowing that nothing has changed."

It was as if Sellers could hear his thoughts, which wouldn't be out of the realm of possibility. Dylan knew things about the world that most people were blissfully unaware of. *You can die knowing that nothing has changed.* Sellers' words hurt. Almost as much as the hole in his side, but not nearly as much as knowing he wasn't able to save Shane. He sat and thought about everything that had happened up to this point. Was this REALLY it? Had he spent all that time and effort to have it all amount to nothing? The thought made him physically ill. Or, maybe that was the gunshot wound.

Dylan could tell that time was running out and he'd soon be dead. He was getting weaker by the second. A sudden rush of panic hit him as he looked down at the pool of blood that was rapidly growing beneath him. *This is it*, he thought. *This is how I die.* The edges of his vision were beginning to turn dark. *I was so close. I'm sorry I couldn't help you Shane.* As Dylan's vision began to dim, the feeling of panic faded, and a sense of calm took its place. *At least I get to see my parents again.* Then everything went black.

1

BEGINNINGS

When Greg Ayers turned the corner and ran into Miranda Russell, the Denver Broncos had just scored and Greg was rushing back to his seat to check out the replay on the stadium's Jumbotron. Mortified, he grabbed some napkins to help clean up the beer and nachos he had knocked from her hands, and he apologized over and over again. He offered to buy her another round, which she accepted. The first thing Greg noticed about Miranda was her dazzling light green eyes. He was taken aback by her beauty and fumbled with his words, which Miranda thought was very endearing. She could tell that even though he was a little shy, he was a well educated, kind man. She thought he was quite handsome and there was an instant attraction. They spent nearly the whole game talking to each other. By the time the game was over, they were quite enamored with each other. They exchanged phone numbers and went their separate ways.

Greg called Miranda the following week and asked her on a date. He took her on a walk through the Denver Botanic Gardens and, afterwards, they ate at Pete's Kitchen, a small diner nearby. The next week, he asked her on another date and then another. They were falling for each other.

Greg had just been hired on to the police department straight out of the academy, and Miranda followed him to Castle Rock, the small idyllic suburb south of Denver and she took a job as a cashier at Safeway. They moved into an apartment together, which caused an uproar within their families, as in those days you didn't live together until you were married. But, they explained to their parents that they were adults, they were in love, and they always would be. Their parents reluctantly gave their blessings.

Three years later, on a warm, peaceful evening in the summer of 1982, they were married at the Eisenhower Chapel in Denver. They were madly in love, and it showed. It was a small, beautiful ceremony with their friends and family, and they were happier than they had ever been. The guests spent the night dancing, telling stories about the bride and groom, and everyone was buzzing from the feeling of love in the air. They toasted the bride and groom, and Greg's Best Man made a drunken, rambling speech and everyone laughed. Miranda's Maid of Honor gave a tearful, heartfelt speech congratulating the new couple, and wishing them the happiest of lives. There wasn't a dry eye in the reception hall. It truly was a fairytale beginning.

Shortly after the wedding, they bought a house on Shannock Ave. in Castle Rock, and were excited to start a new family. Six months later, Miranda was overjoyed to announce to her friends and family that she and Greg would be having a child. They were showered with love and support, and another nine months later, in the summer of 1984, Dylan was born.

DYLAN GREW up in a nice neighborhood in the southeast corner of Castle Rock, across the street from Flagstone Elementary School, where he would eventually go to school. They lived in a blue, one story house, with a huge backyard that Dylan would play in. They had friendly neighbors, weekend barbecues and a yearly Fourth of July block party. They were living the American Dream.

Dylan was a handsome young boy, with jet black hair and striking green eyes, just like his mother. When they were out grocery shopping or taking a walk to the neighborhood park to play, strangers would stop them and compliment her on how handsome her little boy was. She always thanked them kindly. He was small for his age, but the doctors said that it was normal, and that he would likely grow up to be one of the bigger kids in school. This turned out to be true. By junior high, he would be the tallest boy in his class.

He was very shy while growing up, which made it difficult to make friends, but he did have one good friend, his next door neighbor, Sam Robinson. They would play in the yard while their mothers sipped lemonade and gossiped. Sam and Dylan would make mud pies in Sam's backyard, play with Sam's dog, an Australian Shepherd named Milo, and they made rudimentary sculptures with Play-Doh in Dylan's living room. Dylan loved to play with his G.I. Joes and Army Men in his backyard, and would often come in after he was done, tracking dirt and mud throughout the house. Miranda would get frustrated, but she loved him more than anything in the world, and would quickly forgive him. It was everything a young boy could want.

DYLAN STARTED kindergarten at Flagstone Elementary in September of 1989. During his first Back-to-School Night, they visited his classroom that had finger paintings, dioramas and other art done by the students hanging on the walls. His teacher, Ms. Russo, stood in the corner of the room greeting parents. When Greg and Miranda walked up to introduce themselves, she told them that Dylan was one of the brightest students she'd ever had.

"Dylan is already able to read three and, sometimes even, four letter words!" Ms. Russo said excitedly. "Most of my other students are just chewing on the books! He's definitely headed for big things. Dylan has a bright future ahead of him."

Greg and Miranda thanked her for the compliments and went around the classroom, meeting some of the other parents. They made several friends that night.

GREG AND MIRANDA were beaming with pride when they got home from his Back-to-School Night. They decided to go to dinner at The Old Stone Church, one of the nicer restaurants in town, and then they would take Dylan to get a toy of his choice at Toys R' Us.

After dinner, the Ayers stopped by Toys R' Us so Dylan could pick out his toy. He went straight to his favorite section: the one with G.I. Joes and Army Men. There was a man seated at a small table next to the aisle. He was in his fifties, with graying hair and a short, well groomed, gray beard.

"Hello young man. Do you like to play with the Army Men?" asked the man at the table.

Dylan's face turned bright red, and he turned around and put his face in between his mother's legs to hide.

Miranda looked at the man, smiled, and apologized. "I'm sorry, he can be a little shy."

"Oh, it's no problem at all. I've got a young boy myself, and he's also quite shy. What's the little guy's name?"

"This is Dylan," Miranda said with the pride of a mother in her voice. She looked down at Dylan, who was still hiding between her legs, and said,"It's okay. You can talk to him."

Dylan gave him a sheepish grin, but still would not open his mouth to say hello.

"Well, if Dylan likes to play with toys, I work with a toy testing company. We are always looking for young boys and girls to come test out our new toys."

He handed Miranda a business card. She looked at it, and it read:

THE DENVER TOY HOUSE
ERIC WALLACE
RECRUITER

"We also compensate mommy and daddy for their time," he said, looking back and forth between Greg and Miranda. Turning his attention to Dylan, he said, "Would you like to come play with some brand new toys that no one has ever played with before? It would really help us out."

Dylan's demeanor relaxed slightly at the mention of brand new toys. He gave another sheepish grin and slowly nodded his head up and down.

Greg cleared his throat, drawing attention to himself and asked, "Just curious, but how much compensation are we talking about here?"

"Good question sir, and I think you'll like the answer. We pay out $100 per session, plus Dylan here gets to keep whatever toy he liked best. You would bring Dylan in for a one hour play time session where he would play with a few other kids his age, and our observers watch from behind a two way mirror to see how they react to certain toys. After the hour is up, each child is paired with one of our associates who then talk with the kids for about 30 to 40 minutes about which toys they liked best, which ones they liked least, and a few other related questions. Then we cut you a check, Dylan picks out the toy he'd like to take home, and you're on your way. Easy as that!"

Greg stared at Mr. Wallace with a look of doubt on his face. "$100 just to play with some toys? Sounds too good to be true. What's the catch?"

"No catch at all, sir. In fact, we allow each tester to come in once a week. We have a constant stream of prototypes coming out, and we want to make sure we are selling the best toys that money can buy."

"What do you think, Miranda? We can definitely use an extra $400 a month."

Miranda looked down at Dylan. "Well what do you think Dylan? Would you like to go test out some toys? You can add to your collection at home."

Dylan nodded his head up and down with glee. He had left the comfort of his mother's legs and was now excitedly checking out all the toys on the man's desk. He reached for a red race car sitting on the desk, but the man stopped him.

"Not yet young man," he said with a kind voice. "You've got to come play with the toys we have at our facility to get a freebie. These are just for show, but we do have these cars and a whole bunch more if your mom decides to bring you. I'm sure your mommy and daddy were going to buy you something new right now though, weren't you mom and dad?" He gave them a sly wink.

"Go ahead and call the phone number on the back of that card I gave you, and set up an appointment with one of our secretaries. We look forward to seeing you soon Dylan! Have a great day folks!"

Greg and Miranda looked at each other excitedly as they followed Dylan into the G.I. Joe section and waited for Dylan to pick out his new toy. An extra $400 a month? This was going to be a life changer. They wouldn't have to worry about their bills as much anymore with some extra spending money coming in. They both silently thought to themselves about all the possibilities as they walked Dylan up to the register. Things were about to change for the better.

2

THE DENVER TOY HOUSE

Miranda made an appointment for the following Saturday, and they were now on their way to The Denver Toy House testing facility in downtown Denver. Dylan sat in his car seat, thinking excitedly about all the cool toys he was about to play with. Miranda was dreaming about what they would use the extra money for with the same child-like enthusiasm. As they travelled down the I-25 towards Denver, Dylan asked his mom questions about what they would be doing.

"Mommy, where are we going again? Is it the toy place?"

"It sure is honey. Once we get there, you'll be going with some nice people who will take you into a room, and then you'll be playing with some other boys and girls. You'll get to play for a whole hour. When you're done, they'll ask you about which toys you liked best. Does that sound like fun?"

"Yeah! Mommy, what kind of toys will they have there? Are they going to have boy toys? I hope they don't have girl toys like dolls."

"I'm sure they'll have toys for everyone sweetie. Mr.

Wallace said that they make all kinds of toys. I'm sure they'll have army men, cars, games...all kinds of fun stuff."

"I hope so," Dylan said quietly.

They pulled up to the nondescript red brick building with a sign that read

THE DENVER TOY HOUSE

in large block lettering on the front of the building. They parked the car, walked up to the front doors and walked inside. The lobby was in a large open area, and it was decorated with oversized models of toys and pictures of children playing with toys hung up on the walls. Miranda and Dylan walked up to the receptionist desk.

"Hi, we're here for an appointment for my son Dylan."

"Let me see. Ahh, yes here we are. How are you Mrs. Ayers? I'll go ahead and let our Head of Operations, Mr. Bryant, know that you're here. He likes to meet the new testers and explain the process to the parents. So go ahead and take a seat, and he'll be with you shortly."

Ten minutes later, the door leading to the back offices opened, and a man walked out. He was a tall man with well manicured, light blonde hair, clean shaven and in very good shape. He had a commanding presence, and she could tell that he was the one in charge of the facility.

"Hello Mrs. Ayers!" he said with enthusiasm. "It's so nice to finally put a face to the name! Hello Dylan! How are you, young man?"

Dylan retreated to his safe space, his mother's legs, and gave the man a meek smile.

He chuckled. "Ahh, we've got a shy one I see. That's all right. We'll have Dylan coming out of that shell in no time. Anyways, my name is Mr. Bryant, but you can call me John if you'd like. I'm the Head of Operations here at The Denver Toy House. So, here's how it works: I'm going to bring little Dylan into the back where we have our big playroom. He will be playing for about an hour with some other young boys and girls, and then he'll be paired up with one of our associates to answer some questions about which toys he liked best, which ones he liked the least, and why. The whole process usually takes about an hour and a half. So Mrs. Ayers, after I take you guys on a quick tour of the facility, you can hang out in the lobby and read a book, or head downtown and take a look around. Maybe grab a quick bite to eat. Whatever you'd like."

"Okay, sounds good Mr. Bryant," Miranda said. "Lead the way."

Mr. Bryant led Dylan and Miranda through the various sections of the building, pointing out all the different rooms along the way. There was the large playroom with about 10 children playing in it, the rows of cubicles where the kids would be interviewed about their playtimes, the factory floor where a good portion of the toys were being manufactured, and finally, the room that had all the different toys that Dylan would potentially be playing with. Dylan's eyes lit up when they entered the room. It was as if he had died and gone to heaven. The room was stacked floor to ceiling with every toy a young boy could ever want and more. On one side of the room, there were boxes of Pogs, piles of Furbys, Beanie Babies and G.I. Joes. On the opposite side, there were race cars, race tracks for the cars, model airplanes, and Nerf Guns. He could stay in the room for hours and never run out of something to play with.

"So there you have it Mrs. Ayers. Pretty basic stuff we're doing here. Go ahead and follow this hall back out to the lobby, and I'll take Dylan here to the back to get the process started. Any questions for me before you head out?"

"Not really. You've covered everything pretty well. The facility seems great, and I think Dylan is going to have a great time. I think I'll head downtown for a while and look around. Dylan, go ahead with Mr. Bryant here. He'll take you to meet some nice friends and play with some toys! Mommy will be back soon, and we can go get some lunch. Maybe even some ice cream afterwards if you're a good boy."

Dylan didn't move for a few seconds and then reluctantly walked over to Mr. Bryant, looking at Miranda the whole time with a look of fear in his eyes.

"Oh Dylan, don't give me those eyes. You're making mommy sad. I promise you will be okay with Mr. Bryant. Remember, you'll get a brand new toy when you're done. And if you're good, we can get that ice cream after lunch!"

Dylan relaxed at the thought of a new toy and ice cream. He waved goodbye to his mom, looked up at Mr. Bryant, smiled, and bravely said, "Okay. Let's go."

Mr. Bryant sat Dylan down in a small, drab, featureless room on a small plastic folding chair. He pulled up his own chair, faced Dylan, and grabbed a file from the counter next to him. He read over it silently for several minutes, looking up at Dylan every few seconds, and finally put the file back on the counter.

"Okay Dylan. I'm going to have one of our doctors come look at you and make sure you are healthy, and then we will take you to go play with the other boys and girls. Does that sound okay?"

Dylan nodded his head, but stared at Mr. Bryant with a worried look on his face.

Mr. Bryant took notice of Dylan's worried demeanor and

said, "Don't worry Dylan. We aren't going to be giving you shots or anything. Our doctor will just come in and check your ears and eyes, check your heartbeat, and make sure you aren't sick. I promise nothing will hurt. Now I'm going to go ahead and leave you here, and Dr. Bissett will be here in just a few minutes. Okay buddy?"

Dylan gave a weak smile and nodded his head. Feeling satisfied with Dylan's non-verbal answer, Mr. Bryant turned and walked out of the room.

As he shut the door, Mr. Bryant turned to the young man in a lab coat standing across the hall and gestured for him to follow. They walked down the dimly lit hallway and came to a door that read:

AUTHORIZED PERSONNEL ONLY

After Mr. Bryant ran his I.D. badge through the reader, they walked through the door into a fairly large conference room with a large desk in the middle. Several other people in lab coats were seated at the table, waiting for Mr. Bryant to sit down at the head of the table.

"Okay everyone, listen up. Our new subject is down the hall waiting for his preliminary tests. Dr. Bissett, when we are done here, you can go ahead and administer the sedatives and take his vitals. His name is Dylan Ayers, and he's six years old. Today will be his first round of hypnosis, and we will give him some of the initial subliminal messages and plant the false memories of his playtime. Does anyone have any questions?"

He looked around the room for several seconds to see if anyone had any questions, but no one seemed to have any.

"No? Okay, let's get to it."

AFTER DYLAN WAITED for what he thought was forever, Dr. Bissett walked into the examination room. He was an older man with white hair and bushy eyebrows, and Dylan thought he smelled like his grandpa: a little like cigarettes and Old Spice. He smiled at Dylan and looked at his chart.

"Hello Dylan! Very nice to meet you. My name is Dr. Bissett, and I'm going to give you your examination today before you get to go play with all the fun toys. Are you excited? I bet you are. So, first things first. Here's a small cup of medicine you can take so we can make sure you are nice and strong."

He handed Dylan the small paper cup, which was actually filled with a strong sedative, and Dylan put it to his mouth and drank it. His face scrunched up from the bitterness, and the doctor gave him another cup filled with water. Dylan quickly emptied the cup to get the taste out of his mouth.

"Okay, great Dylan. Such a big boy. Well, next I'm going to go ahead and take your temperature, and listen to your heart. And after that, I'll take this little instrument here and look inside your ears. Does that sound okay?"

Dylan nodded his head, and Dr. Bissett started with the examination. Dylan started to feel a little sleepy, and yawned. The need to close his eyes got stronger and stronger. As Dr. Bissett was talking and checking his ears, Dylan slowly laid down on the examination table and fell asleep.

DYLAN WOKE up and looked around. He was in a long room with several beds lined up along each side. He sat up, trying to make sense of where he was, and the door opened. A young lady walked in and smiled at Dylan.

"Hi Dylan! You're awake! You had so much fun playing with the other boys and girls that you tuckered yourself right out. You fell asleep during our question time. Did you get a good nap?"

Dylan vaguely remembered playing with some other kids, but it was a blurry memory. He nodded his head to let the lady know that he had a nice nap, though he didn't remember going to sleep. He shook his head groggily and stood up.

The young lady walked him to another room that was full of toys and had Dylan pick out the one that he liked best. He had a very fuzzy memory of playing with a G.I. Joe Army tank, so he picked one out from the group of toys in front of him. The lady took him by the hand and walked him out to the lobby where he was greeted by Miranda.

"Hi Dylan! Did you have fun? Oh! I see you picked out an Army tank. That's so cool!" Miranda looked at the young lady. "Did he do good? He's usually pretty shy around other kids. I hope he wasn't too bad."

"Oh no, he was perfectly fine! He played so hard he wore himself out and fell asleep during the question phase. But don't worry, that's perfectly normal on the first day. It can be a lot more excitement than they're used to. Go ahead and see Susan at the front desk, and she'll write you your check. Then you can be on your way. If you want to bring him back next week, go ahead and make an appointment with her too. We tend to fill up pretty fast, so you might want to do it today. Bye Dylan!"

Miranda walked with Dylan to the front desk, and Susan wrote her the check. She made an appointment for the following week. As Miranda and Dylan walked out of the front door, Dylan was still trying to piece together the events of the day.

DR. BISSETT KNOCKED on the door to Mr. Bryant's office. After he heard him give permission to enter, he opened the door. Mr. Bryant was sitting behind his large oak desk, staring out of a large window at the buildings of downtown Denver.

"Take a seat Dr. Bissett."

The doctor walked forward and sat at the desk as Mr. Bryant slowly turned around.

"I take it that everything went off without a hitch, doctor?"

The doctor looked at him nervously and answered, "Yes Agent Sellers. Everything went perfectly. He had the opening round of hypnosis and subliminal messages. Then we implanted the false memories. He was told that he fell asleep during the questioning process, and he seemed to remember it that way. His mother just picked him up, and she made an appointment for next week. He seems to be a viable candidate sir."

Mr. Bryant was actually Agent Sellers of the A.I.M. Agency: a shadowy mind control program that he started after the C.I.A. program he worked for in the 70's had broken apart. He had started his own program in 1982 with the financial help of several wealthy donors he had met while working for the C.I.A. They would recruit young children at toy stores and group homes, prepare them for training, and when they reached adulthood, they would turn them into sleeper assassins. A.I.M. would assassinate anyone for anybody in the world, as long as they paid. Once their fee was paid, they would activate one or more of their assassins, and the deed would be carried out.

They worked for some of the world's worst criminal enterprises such as the Italian Mob, the Yakuza, the Triads and the Russian Mob. They would double cross, or sometimes even triple cross if the other side found out and paid them more. They weren't above working for the good guys either. Every now and then they would receive a contract from one of his old contacts in the C.I.A. It's been rumored that A.I.M. was responsible for the assassinations of several prominent dictators during the 1980's.

"Excellent doctor. Go ahead and prep for the next candidate coming in. He should be here in the next 20 minutes. Check the files, but I believe his name is Shane. Shane Bennett."

"Yes sir. I'll get right on it."

The doctor left the room, and Agent Sellers turned back around to stare out at the city again. He had built this program from the ground up after losing everything. He thought about how he had gotten here. He was once a promising FBI agent, one of the youngest the Agency had ever seen, and now he was building his own private army of mindless, merciless assassins. The only people who knew about it were the donors and his agents, and they would never talk to the authorities because he had dirt on every single one of them. He was unstoppable.

3

DANTE SELLERS

Dante Sellers was born in the fall of 1950 in the small town of Tellico Plains, Tennessee. He grew up like most kids that live in the rural areas of the south. He'd go fishing at Shortsfoots Pond or Quarry Creek. Sometimes he'd go exploring in the backwoods with his friends. When he was really good, his father would take him on a hunting trip. Those were the days he cherished the most.

Dante was an extremely bright young man, and was moved up to the next grade several times. He was his school's valedictorian, and he graduated at the age of 16 from Tellico Plains High. He was the first person in Tellico Plains to ever do so. At 17 years old, he was accepted to Northeastern University with a full ride scholarship. Four years later, he graduated at the top of his class with a degree in Criminal Justice, and was recruited straight into the FBI in 1970 at the young age of 20.

Dante was stationed at the Cincinnati Field Office for his first assignment. He moved into the Deerpark neighborhood nearby, a quaint little suburb with beautiful houses and friendly people. A week later, once he was all settled in, he started work as an F.B.I. Agent. He was a very promising young man, and had closed several cases in his first year. He was making a name for himself in the intelligence community, and people were taking notice.

In 1972, while getting lunch down the street from his office, he was approached by a middle aged man in a dark suit and sunglasses. Dante looked up from his newspaper as the man sat down at his table.

"Umm, excuse me. Can I help you sir?" asked Dante.

"Agent Dante Sellers?"

"Yes. That's me. What's this about?"

"My name is Special Agent Randall with the C.I.A. We've taken notice of your work, and would like to offer you a position at the Agency. Here's my card. Call the number, and ask for me. We look forward to working with you."

Before Dante was able to even ask a question, the man got up from his seat, turned around and walked away.

"Sir! I have some questions!"

The man ignored him, and Dante got up to follow him down to the end of the block. When he turned the corner, the man was nowhere to be seen. Confused, Dante walked back to his table, finished his lunch, and headed back into work. *Was that guy for real? Were the guys at the office just playing a prank on me?* These questions and more kept running through his head for the rest of the day.

Two weeks later, Dante's curiosity got the better of him, so on his day off, he called the number on the card he was given. The line clicked, and a man answered.

"This is Special Agent Randall. How may I help you?"

"Hi, this is Agent Sellers with the F.B.I. You gave me

your card a few weeks ago, and said to call you. You ran away before I could ask you any questions."

"Yes, yes. Agent Sellers. Well, I'm here now, so ask away."

"Well, you said you were from the C.I.A. I'm pretty happy with my job here at the F.B.I. What do you want ME for?"

"We have been following your career, and you are exactly what we're looking for. Your personality profile matches the program that we want you to join, and we would do anything to get you to come over to us. What can we do to make that happen?"

"I don't know. I'm pretty happy with my job. I love where I live. I've got friends and a life here in Cincinnati."

"Okay, well one thing I can tell you is that the money will be better. A LOT better. As far as your friends and life in Cincinnati...you're young. You can start a new life and get new friends after your assignment with us. The operation is extremely top secret, so we advise our agents to not get too close to anyone. But, I guarantee that this new assignment will be much more exciting than anything you could ever do in the F.B.I."

Dante sat quietly thinking on the phone before answering, "Sounds interesting, but I'm still not sure. Where will I be stationed?"

"You'll be joining our project's headquarters in California. I can't tell you much more until you agree to join, and then we can give you all the details you want."

"I'm definitely interested, but can I take a while to mull it over? This is a huge life changing decision."

"Okay, but you've got three days. We'll be in touch."

Dante hung up the phone and sat in silence for a while, thinking about what he would do. The assignment sounded way more exciting than hunting down white collar criminals in the Tax Fraud department at the F.B.I., and sunny California didn't sound so bad either. This was going to be the biggest decision of his career.

THREE DAYS LATER, Dante called Agent Randall, and let him know that he was going to accept the job offer and take the position with the C.I.A. Agent Randall congratulated him on the decision, and set up an appointment to meet him and be briefed on the assignment.

Two days later he arrived at the address Agent Randall had given him. It was a tall, 30 story building in the heart of downtown Cincinnati. Dante walked up to the reception desk, and showed them the card Agent Randall had given him. The receptionist said it was on the 5th floor, and pointed him towards the elevators. He got onto the elevator with several other people and got off on the 5th floor. He found his way to room 559, and knocked on the door. Several seconds later, Agent Randall opened the door.

"Dante, it's great to see you! Come in, come in. Take a seat, and I'll go ahead and get you up to speed."

There was a round table in the center of the small, plain room. Dante nervously sat down at the table not knowing what to expect.

"Okay Dante. So, here's the deal. I'm the Head Agent for a Program called MKUltra. The program that you will be working for starting today. Have you heard of it?"

Dante shook his head to let him know that he hadn't.

"Okay, well the program has been around since 1953. We are in charge of doing research into various aspects of the human mind, particularly mind control. We started as a response to the use of mind control on our soldiers by the countries of Russia, China and North Korea. We have evolved into using what we've learned over the years to train ordinary citizens to be sleeper agents for the U.S. Now, what we do here isn't exactly "legal" per se, but seeing as you've never heard of us, I'd say we are doing a great job of keeping it a secret."

Dante smiled nervously at Agent Randall, and gave him a half hearted laugh.

"I can see you're asking yourself, 'What have I gotten myself into.' I can assure you, you are perfectly safe, and this will be an extremely rewarding experience for you.

"So, your job as of right now, will be to travel to our site in San Francisco, get settled in, and then you'll be going to college campuses around the area recruiting viable candidates for the testing phase. You'll be telling them that they'll be volunteering to test out a new pharmaceutical drug that's being tested. Most of these liberal hippies at Berkeley and Stanford just hear the word 'drug' and they'll sign their life away."

Dante was second guessing his decision to join the C.I.A. He was nervously looking at Agent Randall, trying not to let him know how scared he really was.

"I can tell you're still nervous Dante, and you don't need to be. I promise. You won't be present for any of the tests. Your sole job is recruitment. I picked you, because I saw how you could get things done over at the F.B.I. You can continue with recruitment as long as you'd like, or in the future, if you want, you can learn more about the testing process. It's actually quite interesting."

Dante sat for a while in silence, and looked at Agent Randall. He went over everything Agent Randall had told him so far, trying to decide if it was something he could do.

After 30 seconds of quiet deliberation, he looked at Agent Randall and gave him his answer.

"To be honest, you're right. I AM second guessing my decision, but I'm willing to give it a go. Recruitment seems innocuous enough. When do I leave for San Francisco?"

"That's what I like to hear Dante! A man who knows what he wants! Go ahead and take the next few days to pack up your stuff and say your goodbyes. Then on Saturday, you'll get on a plane and start your new life in San Francisco. We have a house set up for you already, so we will send your stuff out to you. Welcome to the C.I.A.!"

DANTE HAD BEEN WORKING with the program for a year when it was officially shut down in 1973, because the public had found out through a whistleblower that the government was experimenting with mind control on their own citizens. Though the program never really stopped and it was still up and running, just not in the eyes of the public. The program was now paid for with the Black Budget, money the government puts aside for classified and other secret operations.

He had worked his way up in the ranks in the first year, and continued to do so for the next two. He had become Agent Randall's right hand man by 1975, and he received permission to go visit his parents for Christmas in Tellico Plains with the unspoken knowledge that he was under no circumstances to talk to ANYONE about what he did for the C.I.A.

He arrived just in time for Christmas Eve, and his parents greeted him with open arms. His mother showered him with love, having not seen him in person for years. They had a great Christmas Eve, and they opened presents on Christmas morning. Dante spared no expense, and bought his mother a beautiful diamond necklace and his dad a brand new table saw.

"Oh Dante," hi's mother exclaimed. "This is just too much! How can you possibly afford this?!"

"It's really no problem mom. I received a huge bonus at work, and you guys deserve the best. Consider it my apology for all the times I wasn't able to make it for Christmas. You two are the best parents a person could ask for, and you deserve nothing but the best. Merry Christmas mom and dad. I love you more than you could know."

She kissed him on the cheek, and they continued to have an amazing Christmas day together. At the end of the day, he retired to his old room to go over some paperwork he had brought along to catch up on.

The next morning he woke up early to go on a jog. When he returned, his mom and dad were sitting down at the kitchen table, with his files in front of them. He panicked.

"Mom! What are you guys doing with my papers! I had those locked away in my briefcase! Those are Top Secret files!"

"Oh honey," she said with the sound of disappointment only a mother could make. "I was cleaning up your room and when I picked up your briefcase, it fell open. When I was putting the papers back in, I noticed words like 'mind control' and 'torture'. Please tell me you have nothing to do with the atrocities that are in these files. How could you work for such a despicable organization?!"

"I can't talk with you about any of this. I need to leave now. Please mom, you can NOT tell anyone about this! Promise me!"

She looked away in disappointment as he grabbed the files off the kitchen table and headed to his room to pack.

Dante knew that he had made a huge mistake by bringing those files with him, but he was behind schedule and figured his parents would never see them. Except they did, and now all he could do was just hope that no one would realize his mistake. He headed to the airport without telling his parents goodbye. He couldn't stand the thought of having to face them.

THE NEXT DAY, when he reported back to headquarters, Agent Randall motioned for him to join him in his office.

"Take a seat Dante. Now what I'm about to tell you might sting a little, seeing as you're my top Agent. But, when we let you go see your folks for Christmas, we put a bug in your briefcase. We had to make sure that you weren't saying anything about the program."

Dante's heart sank. He knew what was coming next.

"We heard the conversation with your parents. They know too much Dante. Our program isn't officially sanctioned by the government. If they tell anyone about what they know, we can ALL go to jail. For a LONG time. The government will deny their knowledge of our program, and we will be punished to the full extent of the law. We'll most likely be tried and executed for treason. It was your careless mistake that led to them finding out. You need to go back, and take care of it."

Dante didn't know how to grasp what he had just heard.

"Wait a minute sir. You're not telling me what I think you're telling me, are you? They don't really know too much sir, I swear. They won't tell anyone anything. They know better."

Agent Randall lifted his eyebrows. "I'd love to believe

that Dante. I really would, but we just can't take chances like that. Either you go back tomorrow and take care of it, or we'll be forced to do it for you and you'll become a liability at that point. You get what I'm saying son? You can make sure your folks die a peaceful death, OR we can take care of it. I can promise you that none of your deaths will be pleasant."

"I can't kill my own parents! That can't be the ONLY possibility! I WON"T do it sir! Please, I'm begging you here. I can go back home and explain that they can never tell anyone or else they'll be killed. They'll understand! They NEED to understand!"

Agent Randall picked up his phone and dialed a number.

"Hello, this is Agent Randall. Send over one of our agents to…"

"Okay! Okay! I'll do it! Don't send someone else!"

He felt sick to his stomach. He had no choice. He couldn't let his parents die a horrible death. He'd have to go back to his parents house and kill them. The agency was too powerful, and he wouldn't have a chance in hell to hide his parents from them. He assured Agent Randall that he understood the repercussions if he didn't follow through with this, and excused himself and went back to his office. He sat at his desk agonizing over the situation he now found himself in. Everything in his life had been going great, and now he was tasked with having to kill his own parents. He went over scenario after scenario trying to find a way to let his parents live. He could sneak them out of the country, fake their deaths and give them new identities, anything to keep them alive. But everything he came up with ran into problem after problem. No matter what he might do, Randall would find out and his parents would die along with himself. As much as he hated it, his best option was to give his parents a more humane death by taking care of it himself.

THE NEXT DAY, Dante hopped on a plane and returned to Tellico Plains. The 50 mile cab ride from Knoxville was an emotional hell ride. He wasn't sure if he would be able to go through with it. But he knew that if he didn't, they would ALL die horrible, drawn out, painful deaths.

When he pulled up to his parents' house, his heart was beating out of his chest. This was it. It had to be done. He knocked on the front door, and his instincts kicked in when his mom answered

"Hey mom. I'm sorry I left without saying goodbye, but I was just so ashamed of myself, and couldn't look you and dad in the eyes. Can I come in and make us all some coffee? I can apologize, and we can talk this over?"

"Of course honey. Come on in. You go put the coffee on, and I'll go get your father."

Dante went into the kitchen and started a pot of coffee. He pulled out the small baggie of white powder, and poured a fair amount into two of the coffee cups. It was numorphan, a powerful opioid that was ten times stronger than morphine. His parents would get sleepy, lay down in bed, and die peacefully while dreaming of happy things. He chose it so he wouldn't have to watch his parents die. If he had to kill them, this was the most peaceful option. He poured the coffee into the cups as his parents were walking into the kitchen.

They talked for an hour or so, Dante lying the whole time that he would be leaving his job soon and be moving back to Tennessee. They were overjoyed. As they sat talking, they became increasingly more tired. Dante helped them up and put them in bed, telling them he loved them and he'd see them in the morning. Once he was sure they were asleep, he placed the suicide note he had forged in his father's handwriting on the kitchen counter. It detailed how he had given his wife and himself lethal doses of the drug, and that he was sorry, but he just couldn't go on any longer. Feeling sick to his stomach, Dante went to the bathroom down the hall to vomit, and he left for the airport when he was done.

Two days later he would receive a phone call from the coroner's office in Tellico Plains letting him know that his parents had died. He made the arrangements for their funerals and took care of everything else that needed to be done. He would never be the same again. He had crossed the point of no return, and there was no going back. He had become a monster. This was the moment he lost any humanity he had left.

4

VISIONS

Miranda continued to take Dylan to The Denver Toy House once a week over the next four years. It was an easy extra income, and Dylan seemed to enjoy it. Although, his demeanor slowly changed while he was going to the toy testing facility; he would have bad dreams more frequently than before, and he seemed to be more on edge. Miranda figured it wasn't anything to worry about. She thought he was just a nervous kid. He had never asked her to stop going to the appointments, and he loved having new toys every week to play with.

In 1994, when Dylan turned 10, Mr. Bryant, A.K.A. Agents Sellers, rang up Miranda on the phone.

"Hello?"

"Mrs. Ayers, this is Mr. Bryant down at The Denver Toy House. The reason I'm calling is because I see it's Dylan's birthday today. Tell him I said, 'Happy Birthday'. Anyways, once our testers turn 10, we have them stop coming in for testing. I assure you it was nothing that Dylan did wrong or anything. It's just that our testing shows that after the age of 10 the kids stop showing the same insight into the toys, so we let them go and bring in some new testers. I just wanted to tell you personally that it was a pleasure having Dylan test toys for us. He was always one of my favorites to have here. I think he's headed for great things."

"Thank you for the kind words Mr. Bryant," said Miranda, barely hiding the disappointment in her voice. "I'm sure Dylan will be disappointed, but he's had a great time testing toys for you. Thank you for the opportunity. Greg and I will definitely miss the extra money. That's for sure."

"Well we know that our long term testers' parents rely on the extra money, so we give our outgoing testers a compensation check to show our appreciation. You'll be receiving a check in the mail shortly. Thank you for all the years of testing. It was greatly appreciated."

"Thank you for the call Mr. Bryant. Like I said, I'm sure Dylan will be disappointed, but I'm sure he'll understand. He will definitely miss all those toys. You have a good day."

Miranda hung up the phone. She was disappointed because the extra money would no longer be coming in, but she always knew it wasn't going to last forever. She let out a big sigh, and went to Dylan's room to give him the bad news.

A few months later, Dylan started to have very vivid, strange dreams. He would wake up in a cold sweat, breathing heavily, and he would be extremely confused about what he had just seen.

In the dream, Dylan would be back at The Denver Toy House playing with the other children. Then a door would open on the floor, and a hand would poke out and motion for him to come down. He would look up at the other kids to see if anyone else was seeing what he was seeing. Every kid would be staring at him, unblinking, toys in hand. The hand would motion for him to follow again, and he would have a strong urge to follow it.

He would descend the ladder into the floor and find himself in a darkened room, lit by red lights. There were four large screens on each wall; each of them almost the size of the entire wall, and they would be playing a fast sequence of random pictures, often violent in nature, or a quick succession of words, flashed on the screen so quickly that it was almost impossible to read.

Then a group of young boys and girls would be led into the room, staring straight ahead, expressionless, and they would simultaneously sit in large chairs, similar to the ones at the dentist he hated so much. They would be strapped down by men in lab coats with featureless faces: no eyes, noses or mouths. Just flat, pale skin. A sense of panic would run down his spine, and Dylan would turn around to climb back up the ladder. But, there would be one of the faceless men in the ladder's place. The man would reach out to grab Dylan, and that's when he would wake up in his bed.

He'd have this dream, and several others like it, off and on for the next 4 years. He didn't tell his parents because he thought they might assume he was crazy or that there was something wrong with him, so he would keep it to himself.

When Dylan and his parents were in town shopping at the mall or going out to eat at their favorite restaurant, Dylan would notice men in dark suits, standing at a distance watching him. He would try and tell his parents, but they'd be gone when he'd look back to where they were standing. He would even notice those same men driving by in a large sedan while he was playing with his neighbor, Sam, in the front yard, or playing on the playground at recess when he was in school.

ONE DAY during his first year in high school, while he was playing basketball at school, he fell and hit his head hard on the playground asphalt and everything went black.

Slowly, Dylan's vision came back to him, like he was waking up from a deep sleep. Confused, he looked around and realized he was back at The Denver Toy House and was being walked into the back room by one of the employees to wait in the waiting room. This would happen on every trip there and wasn't out of the ordinary. What WAS out of the ordinary this time though, was that he was seeing things from outside of his body. He watched himself being told to sit and wait for his turn to join the playgroup, and there was a small television playing cartoons while he waited. He noticed that the television started playing the random images and words that he had been seeing in his dreams. He watched as his eyes went glassy, and a man walked into the room. He led Dylan into another room, and seated him in one of the dentist-like chairs and strapped him in.

At that point, Dylan came to, still on the asphalt, with the school nurse hovering above him. She helped him up, and they walked to the office. Once there, she checked him out to make sure he didn't have a concussion, and the secretary called Miranda to come pick him up.

On the car ride home, Dylan told his mom about the vision he had.

"Mom, I had a strange thing happen when I was knocked out. I saw myself from outside of my body back at The Denver Toy House. I saw myself being led to a room where they were showing me these weird pictures and words on a screen. I think they were doing some kind of experiments on me or something."

"Hmm, that sure does seem like a weird dream," Miranda said with doubt in her voice.

"But it wasn't a dream! It felt like I was really there. I've never had a dream that felt this real. I really think they were doing some kind of experiments on me when I was going there."

"Dylan, please. We both know that isn't true. You just hit your head and had some kind of crazy vision. Now drop it young man."

"But Mom! You have to believe me! They are doing some kind of experiments on kids. Maybe if we tell dad, he can tell his boss down at the police station, and they can stop them!"

"Don't be ridiculous Dylan. The Denver Toy House isn't some kind of secret lab where they do experiments on kids. People would know if that was going on."

Dylan looked at her in frustration. He knew it wasn't just a dream. There was just something about it that felt so real. He couldn't explain it in words, but he knew deep down that it was absolutely true.

"But mom, remember all those times I told you about the men I'd see watching me, and you'd never believe me? I know there's something going on. You've got to believe me mom!"

"Dylan, that's not how the real world works. There are no secret organizations doing experiments on little kids. That's just on television and in the movies. Now, I don't want to hear another word about it young man. "

Dylan looked at his mother with frustration and defeat. He sat quietly in his seat for the rest of the car ride home, thinking of the vision and what it could mean.

When his dad got home from work later that night, Dylan pulled him aside and told him about the vision, hoping his dad would understand. He didn't. Just like his mom, he told Dylan it was just a dream, and it didn't mean anything. Dylan didn't know what else to do. If his own mother and father didn't believe him, who would? He went to bed that night not knowing what he could do.

SEVERAL WEEKS LATER, while they were out shopping at the Sears in the mall for some new clothes for Dylan, Miranda spotted a man across the store watching them. Dylan noticed at the same time and told his mom that it was one of the men he had seen following him.

Miranda took off towards the man, and he turned around and started walking the other way. She picked up her pace, and the man followed suit. He made his way through the Men's Department, turned right at Kitchen Wares, and then headed towards the exit that led into the crowded mall.

She yelled out, "Hey! You! Stop! Why are you watching my son! If I ever see you again, I'm calling the cops!"

He broke into a sprint and ran out of the store disappearing into the sea of people. Miranda followed him out, but he was lost among all of the shoppers. She looked back and forth trying to spot him again, but it was no use: he was gone. She walked back over to Dylan.

"See mom! I TOLD you! That was one of the men I've seen watching me. Do you believe me now?"

"Yes Dylan, I do. I'm sorry I didn't believe you earlier. Let's go home and talk to your dad about this. We can talk over our options and see what we can do next."

They left the mall to head home. They sat in silence the entire ride, and Miranda constantly checked her rear view mirrors to see if anyone was following them, not that she believed she'd know if they were. They got home and Miranda called Greg at work to tell him to come straight home so they could discuss what had just happened. She hung up, and she and Dylan sat at the kitchen table, patiently waiting for Greg to get home.

GREG RUSHED HOME, and Miranda explained what had happened earlier at the mall. She told him what the man looked like, what he was wearing, and any other little detail she could remember that she thought might be of importance. Once he was over the initial shock, Greg called his partner, Gary Denman, and explained to him what was going on. Gary said he'd start to fill out a report. He reminded Greg that their small department didn't have a ton of resources, and that he should probably get a hold of their contact at the F.B.I. and see what they could do.

Greg hung up the phone and dialed the number for the F.B.I. office in Denver, and an agent picked up the phone.

"Federal Bureau of Investigation, Denver office. This is Agent Layton, how can I help you?"

"Hey John, it's Greg Ayers over at the Castle Rock P.D. I've got a favor to ask. My son has been seeing men watching him, and he and his mother were just at the mall when his mother witnessed a man doing just that. When she tried to confront him, he ran away."

"Hey Greg. I'm sorry to hear that. I can't really do anything over the phone, but if you can come into our office and see me, you can fill out a report. I'll go ahead and bump you to the priority list, and we can try and nail this bastard."

"There's nothing you can do over the phone John? My kid and his mother are sitting here extremely frightened."

"I'm sorry Greg, but that's what has to happen. We have strict procedures that we follow. You know how it is: red tape and all. I wish you didn't have to come out here, but that's just how it has to be. I'm sorry."

Greg was frustrated that his friend couldn't do anything for him on the phone, but said he understood. He hung up the phone and turned to Miranda and Dylan sitting at the table.

"Well, he said that there's nothing they can do over the phone, and that we have to go into their Denver office to file a report. Hopefully they can get this guy."

He saw that they were clearly still anxious and afraid, so he tried to downplay the situation.

"I'm thinking since tomorrow is Saturday, we can wake up nice and early and take a trip into Denver to file the report. Maybe we can do something out there the rest of the day. How's that sound?"

Miranda looked at Greg, annoyed that he wasn't taking this more seriously..

"Greg, we need to do this right now. Dylan can go next door and hang out with Sam, and we can be out there and back in a few hours. I don't want Dylan to have to go through having to talk to a bunch of agents. I was there and I witnessed it, so they can have my statement. Is that okay with you Dylan?"

"Yeah, I'd rather just stay here and hang out with Sam until you get back."

Miranda called Mrs. Robinson and asked her if it was all right for Dylan to come over while they ran to Denver. Mrs. Robinson said that it was fine, and they'd love to have Dylan over. Dylan headed next door while Greg and Miranda got in the car and headed to make the report at the F.B.I.

A FEW HOURS went by and Greg and Miranda hadn't come home yet. A few hours after that, Dylan started to worry. The Robinsons tried to calm his nerves by suggesting that it was nothing to worry about, and there was probably just a lot of paperwork to fill out. It helped a little, and he tried to convince himself that it was true. As he was pacing in front of the window, he saw a police car pull up in front of his house. It was his dad's partner, Gary. He ran out to meet him, and his heart sank when he saw Gary's face. He just knew.

"Dylan? I'm not sure how to tell you this young man, but your parents have been in an accident. They didn't make it."

Dylan fell to the ground and cried uncontrollably. Gary did what he could do to console him, and he asked Dylan to come to the station with him so he could call around and see where Dylan could go. He knew that Dylan's grandparents were no longer around and that Dylan was now all alone.

Dylan spent the next few hours in a haze, not really sure if this was real or just some kind of waking nightmare. At the police station, people kept coming up to him offering their sympathies. A couple of detectives came in and explained what happened. They told him that his parents were driving on the highway when a hit and run driver swerved into them, causing them to crash and fly off of an overpass. He was assured that they did not suffer, but that did nothing to sooth his pain. The detectives said they were investigating and interviewing witnesses. They hoped to find the driver as soon as possible.

He was told that since he was a minor, he'd have to be placed into a Boys Home since he had no other living relatives. Until then, the Robinsons were kind enough to let him stay with them for a few weeks while arrangements were made for him to be accepted into a home.

He spent the next two weeks at the Robinson's in bed

crying, not sure of what to do. It was like living in a bad dream from which he couldn't wake up. Sam and his parents tried their best to comfort Dylan, but to no avail. They made sure he ate some food and kept himself clean, but that was about all they could do to help him.

Two weeks later, on a Friday evening, a man came to the Robinson's front door and asked for Dylan. He told Mrs. Robinson he was from the New Hope Boys Home, and he was here to pick up Dylan. She went and got Dylan from the other room and brought him in to meet the man.

"Hi Dylan. I'm so sorry for your loss. I know it's got to be one of the worst things that can happen to a young man. My name is Mr. Kane. I'm the man in charge over at New Hope Boys Home. You'll be coming to stay with us until you turn 18. There are a ton of boys your age, and I'm sure you'll make friends with no problem at all. We have our own school where you will finish your studies, and then we have a pretty high success rate of placing our boys into the job pool.

"So go ahead and pack up your belongings while I go over some paperwork with Mr. and Mrs. Robinson. Then we will be heading to Boulder, which is where the Home is located. I know this is a very hard time for you, but I promise you'll be okay once you get settled in at New Hope. Sometimes bad things happen, but then good things take their place."

Dylan packed his bags, scared about going to some strange place where he didn't know anybody and all kinds of emotions filled his head. *What would it be like there? Will I be able to make any friends or will everyone just ignore me?* When he was finished packing, he headed to the living room, said an emotional goodbye to Sam and the Robinsons, and followed Mr. Kane out of the door and into his new life.

5

NEW HOPE BOYS HOME

That night, they pulled up to a large, three story building on the corner of Balsom and Broadway in central Boulder. It was a nondescript brick structure with windows that were lit up from the inside, and it had no signs indicating what it was used for. Behind the main building, running along Broadway, was a second brick structure, much longer than the first. Both buildings were behind a wrought iron fence. Mr. Kane told Dylan that the longer of the two was the Home's education building and training center where they would train the boys in various occupations for when they turned 18, and it was time to leave the home.

Mr. Kane walked with Dylan to the front gate where they were buzzed in. They walked up to the front doors of the main building and stopped before opening the door.

"Okay Dylan, this is going to be your home for the next four years. I'll go ahead and show you to your room right now, and you can unpack and get some sleep. It's late, so I'll give you a tour in the morning and show you how our program works. Sound good?" Dylan nodded his head sheepishly. "Okay, follow me."

He walked Dylan up to the 3rd floor to room 316 and opened the door. There were two beds, and one was occupied.

Mr. Kane whispered, "Go ahead and quietly unpack what you need for the night, and you can unpack the rest tomorrow. The restroom is three doors down on the left, so you can brush your teeth and use the head if you need to. I'll leave you to it. I'll see you in the morning Dylan."

Dylan quietly put on his pajamas and walked down to the restroom to brush his teeth. Everything still felt like a bad dream, and he was expecting to wake up at any minute. But he didn't. He finished brushing his teeth and settled into his bed. He laid awake for several hours, silently crying to himself. His parents were gone, and he'd never see them again. He was stuck in this strange place, all alone, and he was scared. He didn't know what to expect, and he had no one to comfort him. He was truly alone.

HE AWOKE the next morning to the sounds of someone walking around the room. He slowly opened his eyes and saw the boy that had been sleeping in the bed next to him the night before. The boy looked to be about his same age, give or take a year, and he was pulling on his pants. He was a little shorter than Dylan and had short blonde hair. He was skinny, but in shape, and he was clearly in a hurry.

The boy turned and noticed Dylan staring at him, and said, "Hey, I'm Shane, your new roommate. You'd better get up and get ready. You don't want to be late for roll call."

"Roll call?" Dylan asked with confusion.

"Yeah, roll call. You know, they line us up and make sure everyone is accounted for. Now hurry up and throw some clothes on, and I'll show you where to go."

Dylan hopped out of bed and threw on whatever clothes he had at the top of his bag, and they headed downstairs to the main hall. There were around 20 or 30 boys all lined up in rows, with Mr. Kane and two other men with him. Mr. Kane smiled at Dylan as he and Shane took their place in one of the lines.

Mr. Kane began calling out names. Each boy would answer with 'Here', and then they would turn and walk down the hall to a large double door that they would then enter. Dylan looked at Shane, asking with his eyes what was going on.

Shane whispered, "That's the dining room. After we do roll call, it's breakfast time."

Mr. Kane called Shane's name, and he turned and walked down the hall. Once Dylan's name was called, he followed Shane down the hall to the dining room, and they waited in line to get their food. The day's menu consisted of cereal with milk, scrambled eggs, bacon and a slice of buttered bread.

Dylan hadn't eaten since lunch on the previous day, so he was extremely hungry. Shane watched in amazement as Dylan greedily ate all the food on his plate.

"Wow man, hungry?" he asked sarcastically.

Dylan's face got red. He hadn't realized how fast he was eating. He put down his silverware and wiped his face, and waited for Shane to finish his food.

Before Shane could finish, Mr. Kane walked up to them and said, "Okay Dylan, I see you've finished your breakfast. Why don't you head up and brush your teeth, and then come meet me in the main hall. I'll give you a tour of the facility."

Dylan nodded, picked up his tray, and said goodbye to Shane. He walked over to the kitchen window and put his tray down, turned around, waved to Shane again and then headed up to his room.

AFTER DYLAN WENT UP and brushed his teeth, he headed downstairs to meet Mr. Kane. He explained to Dylan that the main building they were in right now included the living quarters, dining hall, and recreation room. He showed Dylan the rec room, where several boys who had already finished their breakfast were sitting around playing board games or hanging out talking. Dylan looked around the room in awe. It was huge and full of other boys playing games and having fun. He was still lost without his parents, but there were a ton of things to do that might occupy his mind and keep him from constantly thinking about them being gone. *This place might not be so bad,* he thought to himself.

"This is our rec room. We've got tons of board games, a pool table, some video games. But, you have to be quick with those; the list fills up right away. There's plenty to do here on your down time. Any questions about the rec room?"

"How often are we allowed to be in here?"

"Well, anytime you're on free time, you have access to anywhere on the property, except for the staff offices of course."

They left the main building through the back doors and walked to the long, brick building behind the living quarters. It was two stories with a main hallway and several doors on either side.

"This is our education building that I told you about last night. This is where you'll be coming to classes after breakfast, Monday through Friday. You'll be in classes until lunch, and then you'll return for two more classes after lunch. After that, you'll do any homework from that day's lessons. Then after dinner, you will have free time until bed at 9:30.

"Weekends you have to yourself, but you must stay on the

grounds unless we are on our monthly field trip. There is plenty to do in the rec room, or there's a basketball court and equipment you can use in our yard. So what do you like to do in your free time, Dylan? Any hobbies or anything?"

"Well, I guess I like playing basketball a little bit. And I like to play video games."

"Well, there's always a basketball game going on during free time and on the weekends. What's your favorite video game?"

"Probably Metal Gear Solid," Dylan said with a hint of uncertainty.

"Ahh, you like the shoot em up games, huh? Well, you're in luck cause we have that one and a couple others for any of the boys in high school to play. So, any questions about the facility Dylan?"

Dylan said he had none, and Mr. Kane walked him back to the main building. He headed back to his room, where Shane was sitting on the bed reading a book.

Shane looked up and asked, "So how'd you like the tour? I know it's a little much to take in, but I've been here for four years already and it's actually not that bad once you get the hang of things. I never actually properly introduced myself, but as you already know my name's Shane. Shane Bennett."

He stuck out his hand, and Dylan took it and gave it a shake.

"Dylan. Dylan Ayers. So, how old are you Shane?"

"I'm 14, but I'll be 15 in two weeks," he said proudly. "How old are you?"

"I'm also 14, but I won't be 15 for a couple months. So, what do we do now?"

"Well, let's go down to the rec room and see if there are any games to play. I'll give you the rundown on the place. You know, all the things Mr. Kane didn't tell you."

They got up, walked down the hall towards the stairwell, and headed to the rec room. As they walked, Dylan thought about how nice it was that he had found a friend so soon, and he was glad he felt an instant connection with Shane. Now he had someone to talk to, someone to take his mind off his parents' deaths.

When they got to the rec room, they found an empty table, and Dylan sat down while Shane went and got a few board games. *This really isn't so bad,* Dylan thought to himself. *It definitely could be worse. I could be homeless with absolutely no one.* Shane got back to the table, and he sat down. Shane set up the checkerboard he had pulled from the cupboard, and he told Dylan about the place as they played a game.

"So it's pretty laid back here. Although we do have to stay within the boundaries of our main fence, unless we go with our group on our field trip once a month. We go to different places each time, and it's usually a fun time. Also, you have to try and stay away from Mr. Mooney. He's that guy over there in the corner."

Dylan looked to the corner. There was a tall man in his late 20's or early 30's, with a dark crew cut and a mustache, glaring at the kids in the room. He looked MEAN.

"Why's he standing there just staring at all of us?" Dylan wondered aloud.

"Well, for one thing, he's on rec room supervision right now. And two, he's just an asshole. He's in charge of discipline, and he absolutely loves to catch anyone doing anything wrong. He's the worst out of all the staff. Just try to stay away from him, and don't get on his bad side. Since he's in charge of discipline, he gives us a beating if the infraction is big enough and he doesn't hold back. He's good at causing pain, but not leaving a mark. We've tried to tell some of the staff, but they don't believe us. They think we are exaggerating, or they just don't care. It's just better to try and stay out of trouble."

Shane then nodded his head towards a man that walked in through the doors of the rec room. The man was short, a little overweight, with a balding head and a brown goatee.

"That's Mr. Waters. He's ten times better than Mooney, but he's still not an angel. He's usually in a good mood, but sometimes he'll lose his cool and yell at us. He's also our gym teacher. Though you can't tell by looking at him."

Dylan gave a small chuckle. He liked Shane. He was funny and easy to get along with. With everything that had gone wrong in the last few weeks, he was still able to get Dylan to laugh. Dylan could tell that, in time, they'd be good friends.

HE SPENT the rest of the day with Shane walking around the facility, getting to know each other better, and meeting some of the other boys that Shane was friendly with. There was Josh, an older kid in the grade above them, who was known as the joker of the home. He loved playing pranks on some of the younger kids. Then there was Brian, who was one of the smartest kids in their freshman class. Everyone thought he'd be a millionaire one day.

But, not everyone was friendly. Shane pointed out a kid who looked like the typical 'bully' from movies about high school. He was tall, built like an ox, and he had a look of anger in his eyes.

Shane noticed Dylan looking at him and said, "That's Chase Barnett. The home's resident bully. He's a junior, so we will have to deal with him for at least another year. Who knows if he'll ever be able to graduate from the schooling program. Just keep your distance. He might try to mess with you because you're new, but just take it with a grain of salt and don't give him any satisfaction by fighting back. That's what he wants, the confrontation. He'll leave you alone if you don't give him any push back."

Shane and Dylan hung out with Josh and Brian the rest of the day. Dylan liked his new friends, almost as much as he liked Shane. They were fun, easy to get along with, and they knew their way around a basketball court. But, he knew Shane would be his best friend during their time in the home. He just felt that instant connection that he had when he first made friends with Sam, when Sam moved in next door. After they all had lunch together, they played a game of basketball, went to the rec room to play some pool and before they knew it, it was time for dinner.

It had been two weeks since his parents' passing and Dylan was still incredibly heartbroken, but he no longer felt alone. He was making friends on his first day in the home, and he felt like he could make this work.

After dinner, Dylan and Shane headed to the rec room, where they sat around talking with some of the other boys waiting for the Saturday Night Movie. The younger boys all headed to bed at 8:00, and the high school aged boys got to watch The Fifth Element, which came out the year before, but Dylan hadn't seen it yet.

When the movie was over, all the boys headed to their rooms to get ready for bed. Once they were done getting ready, Dylan and Shane sat in bed talking.

"So how'd you end up here?" Shane asked.

Dylan's shoulders dropped, he looked down at his feet, and he sat quietly for several seconds before he spoke.

"My parents were just killed in a car crash."

Tears began flowing from Dylan's eyes as he quietly began to cry.

"Oh, man, I'm so sorry. I know how you feel. My parents are gone too. I was at school one day, and got called into the principal's office. I thought I was in trouble or something, but they told me my dad had killed my mom and then turned the gun on himself. I was 11 years old. Worst day of my life."

"Does it get better? You know, the pain?"

"Yeah, it slowly fades over time, but it never really goes away. I mean, I think about my parents all the time, but I've come to terms with the fact that they're gone. I'm not sure what my dad was going through at the time, but whatever it was he hid it pretty well. He always seemed happy. It must have been something horrendous for him to do what he did, so I've forgiven him. But enough of the sad talk. This place is pretty sweet right? We've got good food, a roof over our heads, a soft bed to sleep in. It could be a lot worse, you know?"

There was a knock on the door, and Mr. Waters poked his head in.

"Lights out guys. Time for bed."

Shane reached over and switched off the light, and they said good night to each other. Dylan sat in silence for a while recalling his first day at New Hope. He could tell that this place would be somewhere that he could call home, and the friends he made during the day, especially Shane, would help him get through the loss of his parents. He slowly fell asleep and dreamed of his mom and dad and of all the good times he had with them.

6

TRY TO REMEMBER THIS

Over the next 3 weeks, Dylan continued to get acquainted with the in's and out's of the Home, as the kids who lived there called it, and his new life there. He and Shane continued to bond, and their friendship grew. He attended his classes including Algebra, Science, World History, and English. Dylan had always been an excellent student and he excelled in every class, especially World History. He'd always been into the military, and he loved to learn about the World Wars.

During his second week, just as Shane had predicted, Chase set his sights on Dylan.

"Hey new guy," sneered Chase as he purposely bumped into Dylan. "My name's Chase. You'd better remember it. If you do as I say, I'll take it easy on you. If you give me any lip, I'll make your life a living hell. Understand?"

Dylan remembered Shane had said to not give him any push back, but at the same time he didn't like anyone pushing him around. He weighed his options, and decided his pride outweighed his passiveness.

"Sure Blake, whatever you say," Dylan said sarcastically, looking Chase straight in the eyes.

Chase lost it. "That's it man! You asked for it!" He took a swing at Dylan, but he ducked and the punch found no target, causing Chase to trip over his own feet. He came down with a hard THUD. Dylan jumped on top of him and unleashed his own round of haymakers, but someone quickly grabbed him from behind and pulled him off. It was Mooney.

"All right you two!" he yelled. "You're coming with me to Mr. Kane's office! March!"

Dylan could tell Chase wasn't done with him, but Dylan also knew the bully's ego was broken. Several boys had seen the fight, and they saw a freshman beat up Chase. Kids talk, and soon the whole home would know what had happened. His days of ruling through fear and intimidation were over.

"Wait here!" Mooney barked. He went into Mr. Kane's office for several minutes to explain the situation.

Chase looked over at Dylan and growled, "Oh, you are so dead kid. Just wait."

Dylan just smiled and ignored him. He could hear the defeat in Chase's voice.

"You two. In here, now!" yelled Mooney.

They walked into the office and took seats in front of Mr. Kane's desk. Kane looked back and forth between the two boys several times and finally spoke.

"Dylan, I'm disappointed in you. You've only been here for two weeks, and you're already in trouble, for fighting no less. But, considering it's your first offense, I'm going to let you off with a warning. Do it again and Mr. Mooney will have the authority to give you whatever punishment he deems fit."

"But that's not fair!" cried Chase. "I'm the one who got hit!"

"Quiet!" boomed Mr. Kane. It was the first time Dylan had ever heard Mr. Kane raise his voice, and it startled him. "As for you Chase Barnett, I've had it with your constant bullying and fighting. You are to go with Mr. Mooney and receive whatever punishment he has for you." Chase tried to object, but Kane stopped him before he could get a word out. "That's final. Now everyone out of my office."

Mooney walked away with Chase and Dylan walked back down the hall, where Shane was waiting for him.

"What happened!?" Shane asked excitedly. "Why aren't you with Mooney getting an ass whooping?"

"Mr. Kane said since it was my first time getting in trouble, he'd let me off with a warning."

"What!? That never happens! You got lucky man. But more importantly, how in the hell did you beat Chase in a fight? I've never seen anyone stand up to him, let alone actually take him on and win! You're gonna be a legend around here, man!"

Shane put his arm around his friend, and they walked down the hall towards the rec room. As they walked, kids kept coming up and congratulating Dylan. He felt a sense of pride, and was overjoyed that he was getting all this admiration. He had done what no one else had done before: he had stood up to Chase and won. Chase would no longer be giving anyone trouble. He'd act like he was still in charge, but now everyone knew that was no longer the case.

ON A FRIDAY, after a month of living at the Home, Dylan went with his class on his first field trip. That morning, he and Shane woke up bright and early, took showers, got dressed, and headed down to breakfast. It was a nice hardy breakfast, and they even gave the boys a morning smoothie, which Dylan had never gotten before.

After breakfast, they headed back upstairs to wash up and brush their teeth. When they were done upstairs, they headed straight down to the main hall to take roll, and then the class followed Mr. Mooney and Mr. Waters out of the front doors and onto the waiting passenger van. The whole class was buzzing with excitement. They would be taking a trip to Elitch Gardens Amusement Park in Denver. They all talked with each other about what rides they would be going on and which rides everyone thought were the best.

After about 15 minutes into the van ride, Dylan started to feel tired. He was having trouble keeping his eyes open, and his head kept bobbing up and down. He just figured it was from waking up so early and all the excitement. What he didn't know was that every other kid in the van was just as sleepy. One by one they all laid their heads back on their seat backs and closed their eyes. Soon, every kid in the van was sound asleep.

"Okay Waters," said Mr. Mooney, looking into the back seats of the van. "Everyone's out. Turn the van around, and we can head back."

Mr. Waters got off on the next exit and got back on the 36 headed back to Boulder. 15 minutes later, they pulled up to the back of the New Hope Education Building. It was Friday morning and all the other kids were at breakfast, so there would be no prying eyes to see them unloading the boys. They brought them all one by one to the basement level and strapped them into individual chairs. They gave them each an injection and waited for the boys to come to. The injection they were given was a powerful hallucinogenic that would make them highly susceptible to hypnosis and make their minds pliable during the mind control programming.

Each chair had its own screen, inches from the occupant's face, and it was flashing random pictures and words in quick succession. As each boy awoke, they stared with indifference at the screen, taking in the pictures and words.

Mr. Mooney was strapping the last boy in and yelled out, "Waters! Jump on the computer and bring up the tests. I'm almost done with the preps."

Mr. Waters sat down behind the control room's computer and brought up the test, and sent it to the screens in front of the boys. At the end of each arm rest was a keypad and control stick. As different questions and pictures popped up, each boy started pushing buttons and using the stick to control things on their screens. They were being tested on various combat and survival situations that they were taught under hypnosis. Every one of the kids at the Home had been a test subject at The Denver Toy House when they were younger. They were seeing if the boys had retained the information they had learned or if they had forgotten it. Those that had forgotten the information would be pulled from any further testing and would live out the rest of their days as normal citizens. If they remembered what they had learned, they would continue the program. And, if they had taken what they had learned and unconsciously improved on the information, they would be added to the Elite Program, where they would learn to become some of the world's best assassins. Dylan and Shane would be added to the Elite Program.

Mr. Mooney opened the door leading out of the basement and turned to Mr. Waters.

"When the tests are finished, boot up the Elitch Gardens memory files, and run it on their screens. When that's done, give me a ring in my office, and I'll head back down and help you lead them to the dining hall. And try not to screw it up like you always do, okay?"

Waters gave him a thumbs up and went back to looking at the computer screen. After Mooney had turned around, Waters shook his head and extended his middle finger. Even the staff hated Mooney.

Over the next two years, they ran these tests and many others on the boys. They took them on twelve "field trips" a year, and every time the boys would think that they had a great time, when in reality they were just being experimented on. The only time they left the property was to begin the trip, so that they'd have enough time for the sedatives to take effect and knock the boys out. None of the boys ever had an inkling to what was actually happening.

DURING THOSE FIRST TWO YEARS, Dylan and Shane became closer and closer. They were more like brothers now rather than friends. They considered each other family and would do anything for one another. They were truly inseparable.

One night while the older boys were watching the Saturday Night Movie, Dylan and Shane were messing around in the back of the rec room. Dylan playfully punched Shane in the arm, and Dylan turned to run away from Shane's retaliation punch. As he turned, he ran straight into Mooney, knocking his coffee out of his hand and spilling it all over his shirt. The commotion made everyone turn around and almost everyone started laughing.

Mooney's face got bright red as he popped up and grabbed Dylan by the arm. He squeezed so hard that Dylan yelped in pain. He led Dylan out of the room and into the main hallway.

"Okay you little shit. I've been waiting for you to screw up again. Let's go!"

Shane ran up from behind.

"Come on Mr. Mooney! It was an accident! He didn't mean to!"

"Back off Shane! Unless you'd like to join Mr. Ayers here for some fun in the punishment room?"

Shane knew better than to say another word. He would do anything for Dylan, but what good would getting himself punished do for Dylan? He quietly watched as his friend was led away to face Mooney's vengeance.

AN HOUR LATER, Dylan limped into his room, and Shane was sitting up on his bed.

"See, I told you he was an asshole. I'm sorry you had to find out the hard way. I wanted to try and help you, but I just didn't think both of us getting a beating would help any. I'm sorry man."

"It's no problem man; I understand. Mr. Kane just lets him do this to kids? There's nothing we can do?"

"Mr. Kane said there's no proof. I guess it's easier to believe a staff member than a kid. The best we can do is just try and avoid him as much as possible. I should've realized we shouldn't have been messing around while he was in there."

Dylan shook his head in disbelief. How can Mooney just get away with that? It just wasn't right.

After Dylan nursed his sore ribs and thighs, he laid down in bed. He couldn't get it out of his head. He needed to try and get to the closest police station and let them know what was going on in the Home. If he told them that his dad was a cop, they'd HAVE to believe him, right?

He started tearing up. He missed his mom and dad more

than anything now, and he wished his dad was here to help. He'd probably beat Mooney to death for what he'd done to Dylan.

He laid in bed for hours thinking about how he would try and get off the property to find a police station until he couldn't keep his eyes open any longer. He finally fell asleep.

THE NEXT MORNING DURING BREAKFAST, his chance came. He noticed one of the kitchen staff had his keycard clipped loosely to his shirt. If he could create a distraction, he could grab the card from off the man's pocket, and go hide it in his room until he had a chance to use it.

He turned to Shane and whispered, "Hey man, when I tell you to, start a distraction."

Shane looked back at Dylan, confused. "Why? I'll get in trouble. I don't want to catch a beating from Mooney. No way!"

"I've got a plan to get us out of here. I'm going to get the key card from the kitchen guy's shirt. If we time it right, no one will see it was us who started it. We'll be fine."

"What do you mean, get us out of here?" asked Shane. "Where will we go? It's not that bad here. Sure, we might get a beating every now and then, but if we don't mess around there's no problems."

"Look man, you might be okay with how they treat us here, but I'm not dude. I'm getting out of here, and I figured since you're my best friend you'd want to come with me. We can just get out of here and figure out what to do from there. Maybe we can go to the police and tell them how Mooney beats us. All I know is that we need to get out of here. So, are you with me?"

Shane sat quietly for half a minute, contemplating what he would do. On one hand, they had a roof over their head and three meals a day. On the other hand, Mooney was out of control with his punishments, and maybe if they went to the police, they'd put him in jail and everything could go back to normal.

"Fine. I'll go along with this, but once we are out, we go straight to the police and tell them about Mooney. Now, tell me when the coast is clear, and I'll start a distraction."

Dylan waited until the man with the key card was cleaning one of the tables near them. He looked around the room to see if Mooney or Waters were looking their way. Waters was flirting with the nurse who worked at the home, and Mooney was busy berating another boy for spilling his milk on the ground. Dylan glanced over at Shane and gave a small nod.

Shane grabbed a handful of the mashed potatoes from his plate and hurled it across the dining room, hitting another boy right in the back of the head. All hell broke loose. Food went flying in all directions. A pancake flew through the air and hit Chase right in the face, leaving a circle of sticky syrup. Chase retaliated by grabbing a handful of his scrambled eggs and hurling them in the direction the pancake had come from. Mooney and Waters tried their best to stop the mayhem to no avail.

Dylan walked past the man with the badge who was in full panic mode, knowing he'd have to clean all this up. Dylan was easily able to grab the badge hanging from his shirt in all of the chaos. Once he had the badge, he slipped out of the dining room and headed up to his room. He hid the badge under his sock drawer and headed back down to the dining room where the excitement was just starting to calm down.

"That's it boys! I've had it!" yelled Mooney. "I don't know

who started it, but don't you worry, I'll be getting to the bottom of this. No one leaves until this mess is cleaned up!"

The man from the kitchen had a look of relief on his face, knowing he wouldn't have to clean it up after all.

"Everyone get to the kitchen and grab a rag or a mop!" Mooney barked. "No one leaves until this dining room is spotless. Get to work!"

The plan had worked. He was able to get the card, and now he and Shane would be able to make their escape. He grabbed a rag and started to clean.

THAT NIGHT as he and Shane were eating their dinner, Mr. Kane walked up and put his hand on Dylan's shoulder.

"Dylan, if you could follow me please?"

Dylan panicked. They knew. They had to. He got out of his chair, and Shane looked at him with horror. They must've found out that the key card was missing, and found out it was them somehow.

He walked with Mr. Kane, neither of them saying a word, and they rounded the corner of the stairwell. Mooney was standing outside of Dylan's room with a smirk on his face. Dylan knew he was caught.

They all walked into Dylan's room. Mooney went straight to Dylan's drawer, pulled out the key card, and untaped it from the bottom of the drawer.

How could he possibly know it was there!? Dylan thought to himself. He thought they'd eventually find it, but there was no way they could've known it was there that quickly.

"We have cameras everywhere Dylan. We looked at the footage after today's incident in the dining room. We saw you take the keycard and hide it in your drawer. What do you have to say for yourself, young man?" Mr. Kane asked. "We expect truth and honesty from our boys, Dylan, not thievery and deceit. You are to go with Mr. Mooney, and you will receive whatever punishment he sees fit. I hope you'll learn your lesson from this young man."

Dylan tried to protest and tell Mr. Kane that Mooney was going to inflict PHYSICAL punishment, but Mr. Kane ignored his pleas and walked down the hall.

"Okay Dylan," growled Mooney. "This time I'm not holding back. Let's go have a little fun, shall we?'

MOONEY WALKED with Dylan down the hall. When they came across Mr. Waters, Mooney told him to come along. Waters followed them out of the back doors and to a side entrance of the education building to a door that was hidden by a bunch of trash and tarps. They took a stairwell down to the basement level that Dylan had no idea was there. *Where are they taking me?* he thought to himself. NOW he was getting worried.

What IS this place? He thought when they walked into the room with all the dentist chairs and television screens. *It looks exactly like the room I've seen in my dreams.* Mooney forced Dylan into one of the chairs with the help of Mr. Waters, and then he strapped him in so he couldn't move. He put a strap around Dylan's forehead so that Dylan couldn't move his head, and he walked away.

Dylan could faintly hear Mooney and Waters having an argument, with Waters saying that Mooney was going too far this time. Mooney told him he'd better keep his mouth shut or he'd be next.

Then he heard Mr. Kane's voice talking with them both.

He told Waters to calm down, and to remember who was in charge. Waters didn't say anything back.

Mooney came back into the room with Mr. Kane carrying a bag, and he plopped it down on a table next to Dylan.

"Okay Dylan, let's see what we've got here. What should I start with first? The pliers? Nah. The hammer? Nah, too many bruises. Ahh, here we are, this will work nicely."

Dylan couldn't see what he was holding, and he didn't want to know. He felt Mooney pull off his shoes and socks. Then he felt panic. There was a sharp pain in the ball of his foot, and Dylan yelled out in pain. And then another. And another. Mooney was repeatedly sticking an inch long needle in the bottom of his foot.

"Stop!" Dylan yelled out. "No more!"

"Oh no, Dylan. You see we're just getting started, so you go ahead and strap in. Oh, wait, you already are."

Mooney continued with the torture, and Dylan felt like he just wanted to die. Then Mr. Kane said something that rocked Dylan to the core.

"Dylan, you've been one of my subjects since you were six. Remember going to The Denver Toy House to test toys when you were younger? Yeah, you never played with any toys. You just thought you did."

It's all true then! Dylan thought to himself. *All the dreams and visions were real. People WERE following me. I knew it!*

"I work for an organization called A.I.M.: Agency for the Investigation of Mind control. We would do tests on you and erase your memory, leaving memories of testing out toys instead. Then when you were too old for the toy testing, we had our agents follow you. To keep track of you."

Dylan tried to lunge at Kane, but he was strapped down and there was nothing he could do.

"Yeah, see, you're getting it. When your mom saw one of

our agents that day, we knew she would try and have it investigated. We just couldn't have that. You see Dylan? We had your parents killed. We would've done it eventually anyways, because you're one of the viable candidates for our assassin program. Sometimes we just have to do it early, because the parents get in the way. Like your buddy Shane's parents."

Dylan glared at Kane and spit directly in his face. Kane laughed as he wiped the spit off with his sleeve.

"You're a live one Dylan. I'll give you that. I've told you all this because you're not going to remember any of it. We're going to give you a little injection, just a little cocktail of drugs that will make your mind more susceptible to the memory wipe. You'll stare at the screen here that will show you a series of images and words that will erase everything we want to erase. And poof! You'll wake up in the morning not remembering a thing. You won't even remember wanting to escape or your pathetic escape attempt."

Try to remember this, try to remember this, Dylan kept repeating in his head.

Kane slipped a needle into Dylan's arm, and within 10 seconds, everything began to fade away.

7

A TRIP TO FORGET

Dylan awoke with a start. He sat up quickly and looked around the room. Shane was still asleep, snoring lightly. Dylan felt his shirt and noticed that he had been sweating heavily and he was out of breath. He'd just had a bad dream, but struggled to remember the details. They were right there at the edge of his mind, but he couldn't quite grasp them. His feet were sore, but he didn't know why. He remembered getting in trouble for stealing the key card, but the only detail that he could remember was that Mooney had given him a beating. Everything else was a blur.

He sat in bed trying to remember what had happened, unsuccessfully, until Shane woke up. He asked Shane if he knew what had happened, but all Shane could tell him was that Mooney had grabbed him at dinner time and then he must've brought Dylan back to the room after he went to sleep, because he hadn't seen Dylan for the rest of the night.

After breakfast, they headed to their first class of the day. As he sat in his first two classes, Dylan couldn't shake the feeling that something weird happened the night before. He day dreamed throughout the day, trying to put it together, but he just couldn't piece anything together.

He had the suspicion that there was something wrong with this place. Of course there was the fact that Mooney was abusive, but that wasn't it. *Come on Dylan, think! You know there's something off; you just have to figure it out.* But no matter how hard he tried, the realization was just out of his grasp.

AFTER A FEW WEEKS had passed without incident, it was once again time for their monthly field trip. Except this time it was only five people from their class. They were told that it was a special trip for the top grade earners. The lucky winners were Dylan, Shane, Brian, Dave and Josh. They'd be going on a whole weekend excursion to the Vail Ski Resort. All the boys were beyond excited. A whole weekend skiing sounded amazing. They all eagerly packed their bags on the morning of the trip and discussed their plans, like what ski runs they would go on, whether they thought snowboarding or skiing was better, and who they thought was most likely to break a bone. Brian was the unanimous winner of that award. Even Brian himself agreed. When they were done packing, they all headed downstairs to load their stuff in the van.

Of course, they had no idea that this would not be a fun weekend trip to the mountains. They would not be spending their time on the slopes; they'd be spending their time in the basement of the New Hope education building undergoing mind control, memory manipulation and military training. They were chosen for this "trip" because they were the most qualified for becoming trained assassins for A.I.M., and this would be their first training session.

None of the boys would remember, of course. They'd be under hypnosis the whole time and would receive false memories of skiing up in Vail. They would actually be receiving high doses of a powerful hallucinogen that Agent Sellers had concocted over the past few years. It would make their minds pliable for the mind-control and training sessions.

It was called NDT, or Neural Dissociative Tryptamine. It was like any other hallucinogen, such as LSD or Psilocybin mushrooms, but it also left the mind more susceptible to coercive persuasion and manipulative hypnosis. In other words, they'd receive the training, but with the combination of the NDT and hypnosis they would remember it only in their subconscious mind.

When they returned to the home after the five boys were sedated, Mooney radioed in to let them know they were back. Kane had the staff keep everyone in doors and out of sight while they brought the boys down to the training room. They strapped the boys into chairs, and each boy was hooked up to an IV with which they were given their drug doses, nutrients and hydration. Each boy also received a catheter because they would be in the chairs for a full 24 hours.

They played the hypnosis sequences on the screens in front of them for hours. When they were done with that, they redosed the boys with NDT and began individual interrogation sessions, where they would grill the boys about things they knew nothing about. Their interrogators were trying to get them to crack, which they inevitably would, confessing to whatever they thought would get the interrogation to end.

After the interrogation, they rolled their chairs into a room with absolutely no light and gave them a double dose of NDT. There were infrared cameras in the rooms so the A.I.M. agents could watch the boys as they descended into madness. When they were at the brink of losing their minds completely, they would pull them back out of the room and run a stream of various, ultra violent images and videos for hours on end. They wanted killers with no conscience. Mindless killing machines.

AFTER THAT FIRST DAY, they gave the boys a rest, letting them sleep still strapped into their chairs. They ran the hypnosis program once the boys woke up. And when they were under hypnosis, they began the subconscious and physical training.

They ran sequences of training videos that, under the special hypnosis, would be retained in their subconsciousness. They learned hand to hand combat, weapons training, survival techniques and espionage.

Following the visual training, they let them out of their chairs and tested the knowledge they had learned under hypnosis by having them spar each other in hand to hand combat and tested them in armed combat scenarios. The next training session, they would take the boys to the deep woods and have them find their way back to a rendezvous point.

At the end of the second day, they were strapped back into their chairs and given the false memories of the skiing trip. Then they were given a special phrase, that when spoken, would activate their hidden training. Mr. Kane gave the same phrase to each boy, and only he knew how to activate their abilities. He had learned in the C.I.A. not to trust anyone but himself.

That night, after all the other boys in the house were asleep, they brought the five boys up, under hypnosis, and put them in bed with memories of the ski slopes implanted in their minds.

THE NEXT MORNING, Dylan and Shane ate breakfast, recalling the trip to Vail. They laughed at the time their friend, Brian, had tried to get on the ski lift and had gotten knocked down in front of a group of pretty girls.

"Man," said Dylan. "That must've been humiliating. I kind of feel sorry for the guy. But not really."

"Or what about when Dave laughed so hard he shot his drink out of his nose?" asked Shane.

"God, I almost forgot about that! That was hilarious!"

They finished up with breakfast, recalling story after story, and then headed to class.

At lunch, Dylan noticed Mr. Waters looking at him and motioned to Dylan with his head to follow him. Dylan kicked Shane under the table and said, "I think Waters is trying to get us to follow him."

"I wonder what he wants? God, I hope we didn't break some rule on the trip or something. I guess we should go see what he wants."

They got up from the table, put their empty trays away and walked over towards Mr. Waters, who turned around and walked out of the dining room, motioning for them to follow. When they turned the corner he had just turned, he was standing in front of the door to his office, and motioned for them to head inside. Dylan and Shane looked at each other, skeptical about going into his office alone, but headed in anyways.

When Dylan and Shane sat down, Waters began pacing back and forth, talking to himself. He was mumbling things like 'no, that wouldn't work' and 'they'll find out anyways.' Then he'd stop, open his mouth to say something to the boys and then go right back to pacing.

Dylan and Shane looked at each other. *He has to be losing it, right?* They asked each other with their eyes.

Finally, after several minutes of pacing and mumbling to himself, he stopped and turned towards the boys and spoke.

"Okay boys, here's the deal. This may come as a bit of a shock to you, but you're a part of a secret program called A.I.M. that's training some of you to be sleeper assassins. We've been training you and other kids under hypnosis, so you'll have no memories of the training. There's some other stuff you'd probably rather not know, but everything I'm telling you is a hundred percent true."

They looked at each other with their eyes wide open. *He's most definitely lost it,* they said to each other with no words needed.

"I can tell that you guys think I'm crazy, but I'm telling you...this is for real. This isn't what I signed up for. I'm no saint. When I joined, I knew we would be training kids to be assassins but torturing kids is just going too far. They've been getting worse and worse with how they treat you kids, and I can't let them keep doing this. I'm going to help you guys escape. But, you can't try to go to the police. The head of our organization has agents EVERYWHERE. Once you're out, you've got to lay low somewhere until I get the chance to find someone who is safe to go to.

"I wish I could let all you kids out of here, but it would be impossible without getting caught. I'm helping you two get out because you've shown the most progress in your training and you've got the best chances of getting this to work. I'll come up with a plan to get you two out within the next few days, and then you'll be on your own. Do you understand?"

They both just stared at him, not knowing if he was serious or just out of his mind. While he definitely seemed crazy, it was almost so crazy that it had to be true.

"Wait," said Dylan. "Why don't you just go to the police and put a stop to it? Why are you helping us escape? You could just do it when you leave on your days off."

"Good question Dylan. I can't do it myself because we go through a training program when we join A.I.M. During the medical examination, they knock us out and an explosive implant is placed near our heart. When we come out of the surgery, we are told about the explosive, and if we go near any restricted areas such as police departments, or FBI buildings, it will go off. They do it to every agent once they have knowledge of the program. It's how they keep us in line. Since you two haven't had the implant yet, you'll be able to do what I can't. Now are you going to do this or not?"

Dylan and Shane were beginning to think it just might be true after all. There was no way Waters would just be making this up. They looked at each other and nodded in agreement.

"Yeah, we're in," Dylan said.

"Okay, meet me back here during lunch tomorrow, and we will go over everything one more time. I'll detail the plan for getting you guys out of here."

Dylan and Shane walked up to their room to sit and discuss what in the hell just happened.

"Are we absolutely sure Waters isn't crazy?" asked Shane. "I mean what he's telling us sounds straight out of a Tom Clancy book. Assassins, mind control, espionage. He's got to be crazy, right? We were just humoring him, right?"

"Well, whether he's crazy or not is irrelevant. He's willing to get us out of here, and I think we need to take him up on it. If he's crazy, we can get out, go to the police and get Mooney thrown in jail and everything will be fine. But if he's telling the truth, it might be a little more complicated than that. I say we talk to him tomorrow, listen to what he has to say and act accordingly. What happens after that is anybody's guess."

THE NEXT DAY DURING LUNCH, they went straight to Mr. Waters' office and knocked on the door. He let them in and had them sit down on the couch. He took a seat at his desk.

"Okay, so there's some things you need to know, just in case anything ever happens and you can't get a hold of me. The main facility that A.I.M. operates out of is located in Colorado Springs. It's on the corner of Sierra Madre and Las Animas. It's in a bunker underneath The ABC Supply Company. There's a secret entrance opened by a numeric code in the northeast corner of the building. The code is 1342.

"This is the facility where they train you guys, once you're out of New Hope. This is where Agent Sellers runs the whole operation. There are typically 5-8 trainees and about 10 or so agents there at all times. I've documented everything I've just told you and more in a book, and I put that book in a safe deposit box at the U.S. Bank on Iris and 28th street. Here's a copy of the key to access it if you need to. Also, in the book I've documented every agent I know of for sure and where they are planted. However, you still need to use caution at all times because there are definitely more agents out there that I don't know about.

"Now that you know everything, here's the plan to get you out. It's pretty cut and dried. I'm on the night shift tonight with Mooney, and he uses the restroom like clockwork. He takes his break at 11:15pm, so have your bags packed and bring only the essentials. I'll disable the cameras, and I'll give two quick knocks at your door. You can follow me to the rear entrance where I'll let you out of the back door. From there, you'll run to the very back gate behind the education building, and I've already bent the fence, just big enough for you guys to get through.

"Once you're out, head as far away from the facility as you think is safe and hail a cab. I'll give you some money for the fare and supplies you'll need when you are on your way out. Take the cab to the Trail Riders Motel in Granby. Stay there for a night. After that, grab a few supplies for camping, and head up to Granby Lake and set up camp. Once a day, head into Granby and make your phone call to me. When it's safe, I'll let you know to come back down. There's a payphone in front of the general store that you can call me on.

"Now, if anything goes wrong, or if anything happens to me, stick to the plan I've just laid out. If you can't get a hold of me, stay hidden until you think it's safe. Go into Granby once or twice a week and check the newspapers to see if they are still looking for you."

"Once you feel it's safe, contact the Loveland F.B.I. field office. That's the only office that, as far as I can tell, doesn't have any planted agents. Anonymously tell them you'd like to make a statement concerning Amy Mason. If they don't answer back with 'Amy Mason in Colorado Springs?' then it'll be safe to go to whichever agent answered the phone. That's A.I.M.'s code phrase.

"If it's safe, call that agent right back and set up a meet. Now, hopefully that won't be necessary, but always have a contingency plan. Now head up to your room, and wait for me."

They walked back to their room, not knowing what to say. Were they ready for this? It all seemed too much. They were definitely in over their heads.

That night, they packed some essentials in their backpacks and waited nervously in their room for Waters to knock. At 11:15, it came. They quietly opened their door, and Waters motioned for them to keep quiet and follow him. They descended the staircase and walked towards the back entrance of the building. Mr. Waters opened the back door and...there was Mr. Mooney. He had just finished a cigarette. As luck would have it, he had taken his bathroom break earlier than normal. Mr. Mooney looked at Mr. Waters, then at the boys holding their backpacks, then back at Mr. Waters. A look of revelation appeared on his face. Just as he was about to open his mouth to say something, Mr. Waters punched him hard in the face and tackled him, causing both of the men to fall down the back steps.

Mr. Waters yelled out, "GO! I'll take care of this! Get out of here!"

The boys wasted no time and ran past the two men rolling on the grass fighting furiously. They got to the back fence, and Dylan took one last look back. He saw Mr. Mooney on top of Mr. Waters, hunting knife in hand, swing the knife down into Waters' chest. Dylan knew it was over for Mr. Waters. He pushed Shane in the direction they were supposed to run and ran as fast as they could go. They ran like their lives depended on it. And they did.

8

ROCKY MOUNTAIN HIGH

Dylan and Shane sat in silence as the cab drove up the mountain, heading for the Trail Riders Motel. After 20 minutes, Dylan couldn't hold in his emotions any longer.

"He killed Waters," he said with tears in his eyes. "I watched the knife go into his chest. There's no way he survived that. That bastard killed him!"

"What are we gonna do now?" asked Shane. "Now that Waters is gone, who are we supposed to go to? I didn't really believe him when he told us everything. Did You?"

"Not really. I thought he lost his mind or was just trying to test us. So does this mean they were actually doing experiments on us? Do you think we have some kind of special powers or something?"

They sat in silence for the rest of the cab ride, trying to make sense of what was going on. They were now on their own with no one to go to. Mr. Waters had told them not to trust anyone, that A.I.M. had agents planted everywhere. He had told them that if anything happened to him, they needed to stay hidden for as long as it takes.

Dylan broke the silence. "Let's just get to the motel, and

we can figure out our plan from there. I think we should just follow what Waters said to do."

They had a long ride ahead of them, so they both closed their eyes and tried to get some rest while they could.

THEY ARRIVED at the Trail Riders Motel at 1:00 in the morning and checked in. It was a small, 12 room motel, with a large neon sign out in front. They told the clerk that they were there for the Waters reservation. When Mr. Waters made the reservation the night before, he told the clerk that his son and his son's friend would be checking in, and he would be a few hours behind them because he was on a business trip. The clerk gave them their room key, and they went straight to the room. It was a small room with two twin beds and wood paneling on the walls, giving it a quaint woodsy feel. They both plopped down on their beds and slept until the morning.

When they woke up, they went over the plans that Mr. Waters had laid out for them. They would need to go to the sporting goods store in Granby and pick up some camping supplies. Dylan checked the envelope Mr. Waters had given him, and they still had 468 dollars left after the cab ride. Dylan knew they'd have to budget though, because they had no idea how long they would be in hiding. He hoped what they had would last long enough.

They got dressed and headed to the sporting goods store. Neither of them had any camping experience besides going to a cabin a few times with their parents when they were younger. They were quite nervous about having to survive in the woods on their own for who knows how long, but they figured it couldn't be too hard. People did it all the time for fun.

They picked out a two man tent that was on sale, two sleeping bags-also on sale, a wilderness survival kit, a camouflage jacket and matching cargo pants for each of them in case it got cold at night, a portable water filtration system so they'd always have fresh water, a couple canteens, and various canned foods. They would restock their food supplies as they needed to. They got directions to Granby Lake from the cashier and started their hike to get there..

The hike was about five and a half miles from the motel to the lake. After hiking for about two hours, they finally got their first look at Lake Granby. It was much larger than they expected. There was a fork in the road, and they took the road running east along the shore. Along the way, they kept their eyes open for anywhere that might look like it could lead to a secluded place to set up camp.

A few miles from the fork that they took, they followed a little trail into the woods and a quarter mile in they found a nice, large clearing that was perfect. It was concealed by large pine trees on all sides and away from any structures or other campsites. They unpacked all the gear and set up camp. Shane went off to collect some firewood, and Dylan got the tent set up.

Once Shane was back, they set up the fire for later in the evening, and then relaxed around the campsite. A few hours later they popped open two of the MRE's, small meals in bags that came in their wilderness survival kit, and quickly devoured them. They had an extremely stressful two days and walked nearly 10 miles that day, so they both fell asleep before they ever got the campfire lit.

Over the next couple of weeks, they would pack up and move camp every few days, trying to stick to the woods and side roads as much as possible. Once a week, they would walk back to Granby and buy a newspaper, hoping there would be no stories in it about them and the murder of Mr. Waters. Every time there was at least a small article about them.

They were wanted for the murder of Mr. Waters. The papers said that they had ambushed and overpowered Mr. Waters late at night, that they were the Home's worst cases, and they were likely armed. Luckily, for whatever reason, the police had assumed they were on the run in Denver or possibly Colorado Springs. At least they had that going for them.

On their third weekly trip into Granby to check the papers and restock their food supplies, they noticed a middle aged woman watching them while she was pumping her gas. They had worn sunglasses and had their hoods up like they always did, trying to hide their identity as best as they could. But, it wasn't a perfect disguise. They avoided eye contact and went into the store to get their supplies. They needed to get out of there as fast as they could.

While buying the supplies, the cashier, an older man in his 60's with grey hair and a bald spot, recognized them from the few trips they'd taken to resupply. He decided now would be a good time to strike up a conversation.

"You two have been by here a few times, haven't you? You out here with your parents?"

"Yup," said Dylan. "We're on a long vacation, and they send us on the supply runs. That's okay though, we like to get out of the woods and into civilization."

"What, you don't like nature? That's the problem with your generation. All you kids care about is video games and the like. You need to get out in nature more often, young man. It really helps you get out of your head and relax. Kids your age should be out exploring and getting in tune with nature.

"Actually, that reminds me of when I was younger. I used to love reading poems by Ralph Waldo Emmerson. You ever heard of him? Of course you haven't! He's not in your video games or MTV music videos! Anyways, my favorite thing he ever said was 'Live in the sunshine, swim the sea, drink the wild air'. That's what you two should be doing. Get out there and enjoy nature! Swim in the lake! Breathe in that crisp mountain air!"

Just then, something changed in Dylan's head. He didn't know what it was but something seemed different. What he didn't know, what he couldn't put his finger on, was that the cashier had spoken the phrase Mr. Kane had implanted into the boys' subconscious. He had just unknowingly activated their hidden abilities.

Shane also noticed that something had changed deep within his mind. He shook it off and told the cashier that that's exactly what they would be going to do right this minute. Shane paid the cashier for the supplies, and they hurried out of the store.

Once they were a good distance away from the town, Dylan turned to Shane and said, "Something just happened back there. I don't know what it is, but I felt something change in my head. I can't really explain it."

Shane looked at him and said, "You felt it too? What was that? I thought I was going crazy."

"Maybe it was just our imagination. We're probably just being paranoid. That lady looked at us like she knew who we were though. We were probably just imagining it, right?"

Shane shrugged his shoulders. They walked back to their

camp, thinking silently to themselves about what had happened, and what it could've been. They both knew that the woman back at the store had probably recognized them, so they'd need to stay hidden for as long as possible. They'd have to make these supplies last as long as they could this time.

THE NEXT WEEK when they were searching for a new spot to set up camp, they came across an old, weathered wooden cabin. It was deep into the woods to the southeast of Lake Granby. It looked like it had been abandoned for a while, but it still looked to be in good condition.

The boys cautiously walked up to the cabin and knocked on the door, just in case it was occupied. No one answered, so Dylan peeked through the window next to the front door. It seemed to be empty and was fairly dusty, indicating that no one had been there for a while. It was furnished, with a dining room table, a couch and recliner, and a small television, which meant there was some kind of power, most likely a generator.

They decided to split up and check around the outside of the cabin for a spare key before they resorted to breaking in. After a minute or two, Shane found one underneath the back porch on a nail. They opened up the back door and went inside.

There were two doors, one on either side of the back wall of the living room. They opened the first one and it was a small room with a twin size bed, a small dresser, and an equally small closet. They walked out and opened the other door. Dylan was in front of Shane and nearly knocked him over when he jumped backwards and yelled out in fear.

"There's a guy in there!" he yelled.

They turned to run out of the cabin, expecting someone to be chasing them or at least to be yelling at them. When they reached the front door, they realized neither was happening, and stopped running. Still nothing. Dylan slowly walked back towards the bedroom door, expecting someone to jump out at any time. He got to the door and saw that the man he thought he had seen was actually a skeleton, still dressed in winter gear making it look like a man was laying in bed.

"Ahhh, gross!" Shane groaned.

"I know it's gross, but we need this cabin. It's better than sleeping on the ground. Get it together so we can get this guy out back and bury him."

"I am NOT touching THAT!"

"Come on man. Do you REALLY want to keep sleeping in a crowded tent with a sleeping bag?! Besides, it's just bones covered in clothes. Come on Shane, help me out here."

Shane gave in, and they wrapped the skeleton up in the sheets he was laying on and brought him outside, Shane gagging the whole time. They dug a shallow grave and buried the unknown man.

After they were done with the burial, they decided to look around the cabin and see if there was anything useful that the man had left them. They checked the outside of the cabin first and noticed there were solar panels on the roof with wires leading to a large wooden shed attached to the side of the cabin. They looked inside and found a large generator and a water filtration system with pipes running into the ground.

"Looks like Mr. Skeleton was living out here off grid," said Dylan. "We should try and see if we can get the power working."

Shane went to look around and found the outhouse about 50 yards away from the cabin. They headed into the cabin and went through every nook and cranny for about a half an hour looking for anything useful. They found an axe, a few fishing poles, several gallons of water, a couple of hunting knives, a hunting bow and 20 or 30 arrows, a few winter jackets that Shane swore he'd never use, and the best part of the haul, a .223 Remington hunting rifle with at least 200 rounds. If they taught themselves to hunt, they could be self sufficient for an extended period of time.

THEY SPENT the next few days exploring around their newly found home. They discovered a small river and followed it to a small uninhabited lake. They decided that the pipes running into the water filtration system must lead to the lake or the river. They found several large meadows that would be perfect for hunting when they needed to.

They grabbed all the bed sheets, blankets, and clothes they had at the cabin and brought them down to the river for a much needed wash.

They tried to turn on the generator, but it wasn't working. Dylan decided to try and fix it, even though he had no clue about how to fix a generator. Hell, he didn't even know how to fix a leaky faucet. But after 20 minutes, he tried to start it and...it worked! He had absolutely no clue how he had done it. But he had. He was beaming with pride for the rest of that day.

Things were looking up for Dylan and Shane. If they could figure out how to hunt, they figured they could live out here for the foreseeable future. They wouldn't have to worry about being caught, and they wouldn't have to worry about relying on anyone else ever again. They had this cabin, and they had each other.

9

THE THRILL OF THE HUNT

Their food stocks were running low after a couple of weeks, and they knew they'd have to start supplying their own food soon. They decided it was time to try their hand at hunting. They knew they'd need to learn how to hunt if they were going to be able to survive being alone in the woods for an indefinite period of time. They decided to try out two methods first, before having to resort to using the rifle. They didn't want to draw any attention to themselves, and figured a rifle going off might bring unwanted visitors. So, they would use the bow and arrow, and they would also set up some snares around the cabin to try and catch some smaller game.

For the snares, they read their survival book and it said they needed some wire, some wood to carve the trigger, and some metal stakes. They went through the supplies they found earlier and found everything they needed. They both went a little ways into the woods and started setting them up. Neither of them had ever set a snare in their life, but they followed the directions in the book and, after a few hours, they both had set about ten each.

When they were finished, they made some dinner of canned chili and a box of macaroni and cheese, and then started planning out their hunting trip in the morning. They knew they would at least need to catch something in one of the snares, but they really hoped to be able to take down some larger game.

"What do you think we'll get tomorrow? I hope we can get a deer!" Dylan said.

"Hopefully we get something. My dad used to go on hunting trips all the time, and he usually never came home with anything. It's a lot harder than it seems, I think."

"Wow, way to be optimistic Shane," Dylan said while rolling his eyes. "At least PRETEND we might get something."

"I'm just being realistic. We have to accept the fact that it might take a few trips to get anything, especially since neither of us have ever gone hunting before."

Dylan rolled his eyes, but thought that Shane was probably right. Of course, he kept that to himself. Dylan didn't want it going to his head or anything. They finished up with dinner and cleaned up. The night was a little chilly, so they made a fire in the wood stove and sat around playing cards before bed. They had a long day ahead of them tomorrow, so they went to bed early, excited about their first hunting trip.

THEY WOKE up early the next morning before the sun was even beginning to show its morning rays over the horizon. They made some oatmeal and ate together, buzzing excitedly, eager to get out and find a spot in the tree line surrounding the meadow where they picked to hunt. They got dressed in the camouflage hunting clothes they bought in Granby, they grabbed some beef jerky and some other snacks, and began their trek to the meadow.

They were in good spirits as they walked, and both were hopeful for the hunting trip.

"What kind of animals do they have up here?" Shane asked.

"I'm not totally sure, but I'm guessing deer for sure. But there's probably some bears and mountain lions, so we should keep a lookout for them, just to be safe."

"Wait, there are MOUNTAIN LIONS out here? Should we even be out here then? I don't want to get mauled to death!"

"Chill out Shane. It'll be fine. We just have to stay sharp. They are probably more afraid of us than we are of them. Besides, it's the bears you REALLY have to worry about," Dylan said with a sly grin.

"Thanks a lot man! That really does wonders for my anxiety. Also, that doesn't sound right man. I'm DEFINITELY more afraid of THEM than they are of ME! Have you seen how big they are?"

"Whatever Shane. The chances of us seeing one are pretty low anyways. Stop worrying about it and stay focused. We need to be on the lookout for animals."

They continued walking through the woods towards the meadow. The only animals they saw the whole time were a few squirrels and a skunk. Neither of them sounded appetizing, so they left them alone.

After hiking for an hour, they came to the meadow that they had picked out. There were currently no animals grazing in it, so they marched along the perimeter, trying to find the perfect spot to sit and wait. They came to a large rock, about 50 feet in diameter and around 10 feet high. It gave them the perfect vantage point. They climbed to the top and sat down to wait for their prey.

THREE HOURS PASSED, and they were beginning to lose hope of bagging any animals on their first time out. Shane was getting antsy and rocking back and forth impatiently.

"Dude, I have to take a leak. I'll be right back."

Shane climbed down off the rock, and went several yards away so that he could hide behind a large tree to take care of business. Just then, on the opposite side of the meadow, Dylan saw a large buck wander into the meadow. It had huge antlers and, from where Dylan was, he seemed to be about four feet tall at the shoulders. He slowly turned back to Shane and gave him the international "shush" sign, one finger pressed against his lips. Then he gave him a wave to come back to the rock. Shane began slowly tip toeing back towards the rock. He was a few feet away when he stepped on a twig with a loud SNAP.

The deer popped its head up to locate the sound of the noise. Dylan instinctively grabbed an arrow and locked it onto the bowstring, pulled back the string, aimed for less than a split second before letting the arrow fly.

The deer barely had the time to take two steps when the arrow found its mark. Dead center in the flank, piercing its heart. The deer went down with a thud. It was dead before it hit the ground.

It took several seconds for Dylan to realize he had even taken the shot. He sat there, staring at the spot the deer had just been, then turned back to Shane.

"I...I think I got it. I don't even remember pulling back the bow. Let's go see."

Dylan climbed down from the rock, and he and Shane walked the 50 or 60 yards to the body of the deer. Shane looked from the deer, to Dylan, back at the deer, and then back towards the rock they were sitting on.

"You hit it dead center! That's got to be at least 50 yards! How'd you do that man!?"

"No clue. I don't remember shooting the arrow. I was looking down at you to tell you to climb back up the rock, then I heard the twig snap under your feet. The next thing I remember, the deer went down. It was like I was on automatic pilot."

"That was amazing man! So now what do we do? How do we get it back to the cabin?"

Without another word, or any hesitation, Dylan grabbed the hunting knife from the sheath on his side and began butchering the deer. It was as if he'd done it a thousand times before. Then, without a word, Shane joined in. They looked at each other, in the middle of cutting up the animal, and just started laughing. Not because they had killed an animal, but because they had no idea how they knew how to do what they were doing. Neither of them had ever butchered a deer before, let alone killed one. Here they were, taking care of the task like they were seasoned hunters.

Once they were done, they loaded up all the meat into the bags they had brought along in case they had a successful hunt and headed back to the cabin. They'd have a feast tonight.

WHEN THEY GOT BACK to the cabin later that day, they put all the meat they had acquired in the large reach-in freezer that was in the kitchen. They kept enough for them to have a nice big steak each that night for dinner. It was their first successful hunt, and they wanted to celebrate. That deer would feed them for the next couple of weeks, at the very least.

Later that night, they cooked up the steaks and sat at the table savoring every bite. It was the first time either of them had eaten deer before. They thought it tasted like cow, but it was a lot chewier. It had more of an earthy taste than cow, which they decided was because it ate grass and berries and other natural things, and the cows they would eat would be fed grains. It was different, but it was definitely something they could get used to.

"So, what happened back there?" asked Shane. "How did we know how to butcher the deer? I've got a theory, but I don't think you'll like it."

Dylan looked at him with a curious expression.

"Well, what I'm thinking is...remember what Waters told us? That they were doing experiments and stuff on us? I think maybe they have been training us or something. Like teaching us how to fight, to shoot, you know...how to survive. I mean, how else do you explain how we knew what to do? Or how you were able to hit a deer, in the heart, from 50 yards, without even thinking about it?"

Dylan didn't have an answer. *Could Shane be right?* It would definitely explain a lot. He'd had strange dreams of people doing experiments on him his whole life. He always thought it was just a weird recurring dream, but maybe it had something to do with all of these new abilities he and Shane seemed to have out of nowhere. He'd shot a deer from 50 yards with a bow and arrow, and he had never used a bow and arrow in his life. The weird thing was that it had felt instinctual. He had put no thought into it. *I've got to find some answers.*

AFTER THE FIRST six months of living in the cabin, they decided they should go to Grand Lake, the small town at the northernmost tip of Lake Granby, and check the papers to see if they were still wanted. It was nearly a 20 mile round trip. They left early in the morning, so they could make it back to the cabin before dark.

They arrived in Grand Lake at around noon and found the closest store where they could grab a newspaper. It wasn't on the front page, but they were still wanted for the murder of Mr. Waters. It looked like they might have to stay at the cabin a while longer. They grabbed a new axe and brought it up to the counter to pay for it and the newspaper.

As they walked out of the store, they heard, "That's those two boys they're looking for!" and turned to see several people staring at them. One of the men in the group said, "Quick, someone call the police! Joe! Let's grab them!"

The boys didn't think twice; they turned around and took off running. The two men were on their tail for about a half mile, then the young boys' stamina won out and they were able to lose the men. Once they knew they were in the clear for sure, they took a quick rest and then started their trek back to the cabin. They'd have to stay at the cabin for quite a while now that they'd been seen in two towns near Lake Granby. There would be law enforcement all over the area soon. If they were right in their assumptions, their cabin would be out of the search area. If they were wrong, they'd definitely be caught.

Over the next few weeks, they kept an eye out for signs of a search. Three days after the incident in Grand Lake, they heard a helicopter circling above the cabin. They stayed out of sight until it was gone, but they knew someone would be coming by to check to see if anyone was in the building. They packed up any evidence that they had been in the cabin and grabbed their camping equipment to hide in the woods until the authorities had come and gone. They kept an eye on the cabin from a distance. After a day, they saw some agents walk inside for several minutes, and radio in that it was just an abandoned hunting shack. Once the agents were gone again, the boys stayed in their tent for two more nights, just to make sure the cabin wasn't being watched. When they were sure it was safe, they headed back.

OVER THE NEXT TWO YEARS, the boys stayed in the cabin, living off of the land. They grew more and more adept at hunting and fishing, and they had learned all the different types of edible plants they could eat from a survival book they found in the cabin. It was a hard but simple way of life. Dylan and Shane had both turned 18, and they were no longer kids. They were men now. Young men but men all the same. They were on their own, with no one to tell them what they could or couldn't do. All the time spent together in the woods had strengthened their bond like never before. No longer were they best friends, they were brothers. It seemed like there was nothing that could go wrong. Until something did.

10

ATTACK!

T he cabin's chest freezer was running low, so Dylan and Shane decided it was time for another hunting excursion. During their previous trips, they had found a meadow that had a small stream running down the center, and there was almost always some kind of wildlife drinking from the stream or grazing in the high grass. It was their favorite spot to hunt because it was almost impossible to walk away without something to fill their freezer. That's where they'd be going on this trip. They packed up their hunting gear and set out bright and early the next morning.

It was a beautiful early spring day, so they took their time on the hike to the meadow. The birds were singing, and the crisp mountain air smelled like wildflowers and pine trees. They took in the beauty around them and agreed that they were truly lucky to be out here in the embrace of mother nature.

They arrived at the meadow two hours later and found it empty. They'd need to get comfy and wait for something to show up. They sat and talked for about an hour, and the meadow was still empty. Shane excused himself to use the little boys tree. He walked 20 yards away to take care of his business, while Dylan kept an eye on the meadow. Dylan looked back to where Shane was squatting behind a tree to ask Shane if he had packed any snacks. He noticed a slight movement in some bushes behind Shane another 25 or so feet to his left.

"Shane," he whispered just loud enough for Shane to hear him. "Don't move. There's something behind you. I'm going to slowly come towards you. Keep still."

Shane's eyes widened in fear, making him look like a frightened lemur.

"What is it?" he whispered back.

Dylan just put his finger to his lips and slowly made his way to Shane with an arrow set on the bowstring, ready to fire if necessary. As he was moving towards Shane, to his utmost horror, he realized what it was. A full grown mountain lion.

He tried to not let the horror show on his face as he told Shane, "Everything's okay man. Just don't move a muscle. There's an animal behind you, and I'm gonna try and get it right now."

Shane knew the fact that Dylan wouldn't say what KIND of animal it was, probably wasn't good. The fear and curiosity was killing him, but he wasn't about to turn around and look.

Just then, the cat sprang out of the bushes, and by the time Dylan aimed and fired his first shot he was already halfway to Shane. When the arrow found its mark, the cat was two feet away. Shane spun around when he saw Dylan raising the bow. As the cat swiped at Shane with its razor sharp claws, it connected with his left thigh. The arrow found its mark, the creature's heart, and it fell to the ground. It let out a final raspy breath and died.

Dylan was at Shane's side in a second, and he instinctively tore off his own shirt and made a tourniquet to stop the bleeding. He pulled Shane's shirt off and wrapped it around the wound.

"Dylan! It got me! Am I going to die? I don't want to die like this man! I'm too young!"

"No Shane, you'll be fine," he said calmly. "I'm pretty sure it missed any major arteries, otherwise you'd be bleeding a lot worse. We are just gonna have to get out of here as quickly as we can, and find a car to bring us into Boulder. It's a risk, but it's a risk we have to take right now. There's a road about a mile from here, so we gotta get there as fast as we possibly can. You with me?"

Shane nodded and put his arm around Dylan's neck, so that Dylan could help him hobble to the main road. It had been a year and a half since the incident in Grand Lake, so they had no idea if the police were still actively searching for them. They'd have to take their chances. Their fate was no longer up to them.

THEY GOT to the road in 45 minutes, and they caught a lucky break. A car was stopped on the shoulder 100 yards away. They rushed towards the car, and a man came out of the woods pulling up his zipper.

"Hey! Mister! My friend's hurt really bad! He was attacked by a mountain lion! We need a ride to Boulder. Now!"

The man ran to his car, opened the back door and said, "Come on! Jump in!"

Dylan sat Shane in the back seat, closed the door and hopped into the opposite side.

"What were you boys doing out here by yourselves?" the

man asked after they were on their way. "Where are your parents?"

"We were out on a hunting trip sir. Our dads have always taken us on trips since we were little. But now that we're both 18, they thought it'd be a good time to do a trip on our own. They're back in Boulder, so I'll let them know where we are once you drop us off at the hospital. You're truly a life saver sir. Who knows how long we would've had to wait if you weren't there when we got to the road!"

Shane had been crying out in pain periodically since they got into the car, but he had been silent now for a while. Dylan checked his pulse and it was slow, but strong. It was another 30 minutes or so to Boulder. They drove as fast as they could down the mountain towards their unknown fate.

SHANE PASSED out from the pain shortly after they got in the car. At first, everything just sort of went black. *Then he found himself sitting in the back seat of his parents' Honda Civic. He looked back and forth at the backs of his parents' heads with confusion. What was he doing here? Weren't his parents dead? Was HE dead? He tried calling out to them, but nothing came out of his mouth. He looked to his left, and there he was: his 6 year old self, playing with the toy he had just gotten from his first trip to The Denver Toy House.*

He blinked and, all of a sudden, he was standing in the lobby of The Denver Toy House. He watched as his mom left the lobby, and a man took his younger self into the back rooms. He followed him into the back and, instead of taking the younger Shane to the playroom, the man brought him to a room filled with medical looking equipment. Then he strapped young Shane into one of the chairs. Several people came into the room and started poking and prodding while he watched himself crying for his mom. He ran at one of the men, intending to do some serious damage. As he swung his fist at the man's head, the room disappeared.

He was now standing in a smaller room where his younger self was strapped into a similar chair with a screen quickly flashing words and pictures on it. There were two men in the room.

One said, "Did you give him the injection yet?"

"Yeah, go ahead and pull up the playtime memories, and run them. I think his mom is picking him up in 20 minutes."

Shane looked at the screen, and the video was in the first person. It was a memory he still remembered. He was playing with the new Teenage Mutant Ninja Turtles action figures he had loved so much as a kid. He had a clear memory of playing with the toys at the testing facility and picking the set as his free gift. He wondered how many of his memories were implanted like this.

Just like that, he was now standing in his old house. It was a sunny day, and his mom walked by whistling "Wonderwall" by Oasis. He followed her into the living room, and his dad was sitting on the couch watching television. His mom sat down next to his dad, cuddled up to him, and laid her head on his shoulder. He smiled, remembering how much his parents loved each other. Then he noticed movement to the left of him.

There was a man standing at the back sliding glass door, slowly opening it. He had a gun with a silencer on it. Shane tried to yell out to his parents to look behind them. Again, nothing came out. He tried to run towards the man, but his legs wouldn't budge. He watched in horror as the man snuck up behind his parents. The man raised the gun, aimed it at his mother's head, and pulled the trigger. His dad turned around and froze when he realized the man had the gun pointing at his face.

"Sit back down!" the man yelled.

Shane's dad, weeping, not knowing what was happening, complied.

"Why are you doing this?"

"It's nothing personal. Your son has been coming to our facility to test toys, but we actually have been testing him. He's been showing aptitude for our assassin program, and he has to start the training. We can't have parents in the way, so unfortunately for you, you've got to be taken out of the picture."

As his dad turned to say something, the man aimed the gun at his dad's temple and pulled the trigger.

Shane heard a yelp from behind him and so did the assassin. Shane watched as the man walked up to 11 year old Shane, who was watching from behind the corner of the hallway. Young Shane was slumped against the wall, tears streaming down his face, in a catatonic like state. The man pulled out a syringe, gave Shane an injection, and his face went blank like he was under some kind of hypnosis.

The assassin leaned in to speak into Shane's ear and said, "Your dad just shot your mom, and then killed himself. This is what you will tell the police."

Shane stared straight ahead and repeated, "My dad just shot my mom and then killed himself."

The man turned around and walked back over to the bodies, wiped down the gun, and placed it in his dad's hand. Shane snapped awake, in a panic. He was in the back seat of the car with Dylan. His leg felt like it was on fire.

"Everything Waters said was true!" yelled Shane. "I just saw everything that happened when I was younger! They were testing me at The Toy House! My dad didn't actually kill my mom and himself! Someone from A.I.M. did it!"

"What's he talking about?" asked the man.

"I don't know," Dylan lied. "He must be delusional from blood loss or something."

Dylan looked at Shane, saying with his eyes, *Not in front of this guy! Tell me later.*

Shane got the message. Still breathing heavily from the excitement of the vision, he changed his demeanor and said, "I must've been dreaming when I passed out. That was a weird dream."

The man must've believed him, because he didn't bring it up again. They were nearly to Boulder. They both hoped silently that no one would recognize them at the hospital.

11

BACK IN BOULDER

They pulled up to Boulder Community Hospital, and Dylan ran inside to get somebody to help. He and a nurse ran out to the car and unloaded Shane onto a gurney, and the nurse wheeled him in. Dylan thanked the man, assured him that everything would be okay and that he was a hero. The man reluctantly pulled away, and Dylan ran into the hospital to talk to the admissions staff.

Dylan walked up to the young woman at the desk just inside the door. She was around 20 years old, had curly light blond hair and a warm smile. She could see from Dylan's worried expression that he was with the boy around his age that they just took back to the E.R.

"Are you with the young man with the left thigh laceration?"

"Yes, ma'am."

"Where are your parents?"

"We are both 18 ma'am. We've been best friends since we were little. Ever since both of our parents died in a plane crash a year ago, we've been living on our own."

She looked at him with a doubtful expression, trying to gage if he was telling the truth or not.

"I'm sorry to hear that. Well, do you have some ID for your friend, so I can check him in?"

"Well we were out on a hunting trip up in the mountains, so our wallets are back at our camp."

They weren't, Dylan and Shane had never been issued any type of identification while they were living at the Boys Home. But, he couldn't let the hospital know that.

"Okay, well what's his name then? And how did he receive his injury?"

"His name's Brian McConnor, and he was attacked by a mountain lion while we were hunting. Is he gonna be okay? Can I go back and check on him?"

"I'm sorry honey, but you can't; they are working on him right now. From what I could tell, it seemed like a non life threatening injury, so he should be just fine. Is there any way you can get a hold of some ID for him? What's your name by the way, honey?"

"Greg. Greg Daniels. Yeah, our wallets are up at our campsite, but our apartment is here in town. I can go grab his birth certificate, if that would be okay?"

"That would be just fine Greg. He should be ready and waiting for you in the lobby when you get back, all patched up and ready to go. Just make sure you bring me his birth certificate, so I can run his insurance, and then you guys can be on your way."

Dylan smiled and said he'd be back soon. The good news was that no one seemed to recognize them, so they must've made it out of the news and into anonymity. Now that they seemed to be safe, Dylan figured it was time that they tried to clear their names. He'd have to call the F.B.I. office in Loveland. Mr. Waters said that it was the only office he wasn't totally sure had any A.I.M. Agents planted in it, so that would be the first place he'd try. He walked out of the hospital and began looking for a phone.

HE FOUND a payphone a few blocks away, and looked up the number for the Loveland Field Office in the phonebook then dialed the number.

"Federal Bureau of Investigation, Loveland. This is Agent Larsen speaking, how can I help you?"

"Hi, yeah, I'd like to make a statement about...Amy Mason?"

"Is that a question, son? Or do you not know who you're wanting to make a statement about?"

The agent didn't answer back with 'Is that the Amy Mason in Colorado Springs?' so he knew the agent wasn't with A.I.M. He hung up the phone, as per Mr. Waters' instructions, and waited a few minutes to call Agent Larsen back.

"Federal Bureau of Investigation, Loveland. This is Agent Larsen speaking, how can I help you?"

"Hi. My name is Dylan Ayers. My friend Shane Bennett and I are probably on a list somewhere for the murder of Mr. Waters at the New Hope Boys Home. Well, we didn't do it. I know that's probably what every person says, but we really didn't. And I have proof. I want to meet you tonight if possible. But, only you. I have proof of an agency that is training young kids to become sleeper assassins. I don't think they are government related, but they have agents planted everywhere, so I only want to meet with you. We will be hidden and if we see that there is anyone else besides you, we will leave. Can we meet you somewhere in Loveland?"

"Is this one of the guys over at the Denver Office? Are

you messing with me?"

"I'm dead serious sir. I have proof of everything I'm telling you. Now PLEASE, where can we meet?"

"Okay 'Dylan', I'll bite. Why don't you come here to my office and we can go over your 'evidence'?"

"I told you already! They have agents planted everywhere! The only reason I knew you weren't with them is because I gave you a code they use, and you didn't respond to it the way you were supposed to."

"That was you? Okay, you've piqued my curiosity. Let's see...why don't we meet at Lakeside Park by Loveland Lake at 8:00 pm tonight? I'll come alone as you've requested. If you DO have proof, we can see where to go from there. If you don't, you have to promise you'll let me take you in so we can get things sorted out. Is that reasonable?"

"Yeah, that's fine. I'll have the proof. It'll be dark out, so wear sunglasses and we'll know it's you. If we feel sure it's you, we will approach you. Lakeside Park, 8:00 pm. See you then."

He hung up the phone and headed back to the hospital. He had to meet up with Shane and try to avoid the receptionist he told he'd bring the IDs back to. Once they were out, they could grab a cab to the bank, grab the book of evidence from the safe deposit box and head to Loveland to meet Agent Larsen.

WHEN HE GOT BACK to the hospital, he entered from a different door than the first time to avoid the receptionist. He found the waiting room and saw Shane sitting there, with a worried look on his face, looking back and forth trying to find Dylan.

Dylan walked up, and Shane motioned with his head to sit next to him. Dylan could tell something wasn't right, so he sat down.

"What's up man? What's wrong?" Dylan asked, worried about how his friend was acting.

"Don't look, but there are two men down the hall. They've been eyeing me ever since I came out here. They've gotta be A.I.M. agents, otherwise they would've called the police or something by now, right?"

Dylan carefully glanced towards the hallway Shane was talking about and there were indeed two men, but they were just in mid conversation and looked disinterested in anything else other than what they were talking about.

"Did they give you pain meds man? You sure you're not imagining things? Those guys don't seem to be interested in us, they're just talking. I've been walking around outside, and no one has been following me or anything. You're probably just being paranoi..."

Just then, Dylan turned his head towards the hallway again and both men were looking at them. They saw Dylan turn to look at them, and they both looked away quickly and went back to their conversation.

"Yeah, okay," said Dylan. "You aren't being paranoid. They are totally watching us. Let me figure out what to do."

"I told you man! I knew they were watching me! What are we going to do? We can't outrun them. My legs are not exactly in the best shape for a sprint!"

"Lemme think!" snapped Dylan.

Dylan looked around, scanning all the exits. The hospital was pretty crowded today, so they'd have some cover if they could cause a distraction.

"Okay," Dylan said. "Just follow my lead."

Dylan stood up and started walking towards the closest

exit and Shane followed. They both watched one of the men tap the other on the arm, and both started to follow the boys. Shane wasn't paranoid then, they were definitely interested in them.

"Okay Shane, get ready to move as quickly as possible when I say."

Shane opened his mouth to protest, but Dylan reached up and pulled the Fire Alarm on the wall before he could get the words out. At the same moment, Dylan said, "Run!"

The alarm started blaring and all hell broke loose. People were running this way and that, panicking, trying to make their way to an exit. Dylan crouched down, with Shane hobbling behind him, trying not to pop the stitches in his leg. They pushed their way to the door that led to the E.R. rooms and went inside. They followed the exit signs leading to the rear entrance. They then ran out into the rear parking lot and found an enclosure that held several dumpsters and ducked inside to hide.

"We can wait here for a little while. Those agents will think we got away and will start looking for us in the streets. They won't realize we're still at the hospital. Once all the excitement has calmed down, we can get a cab to meet the F.B.I. agent I was able to contact. We have to meet him in Loveland later tonight.

THEY SAT and talked about what Dylan had said to Agent Larsen, and they decided what they should tell him. They'd have to stop by the P.O. Box Mr. Waters had given them the key to and pick up the book with all the information in it. But first, Dylan wanted to know about what Shane was talking about on the car ride from the mountains.

"Okay, so what were you talking about in the car on the way down here? You said your dad didn't kill your mom?"

"Yeah man, it was weird. When I passed out, all of a sudden I was sitting next to myself, but a young version of me, in my parents car, and I was playing with a toy I had just got at the toy testing facility they used to take me to."

Dylan's eyes widened. "Wait! YOU used to test toys too? Don't tell me. The Denver Toy House?!"

"How could you possibly..."

"I used to go there too!" Dylan interrupted. "This is all starting to make more sense now! Waters told us we were being experimented on, but I thought he just meant at the Home. Anyways, go ahead and finish your dream."

Shane sat slack jawed for a few seconds and then continued to tell Dylan everything that he had seen in the dream. When he was finished, Dylan sat quietly for several seconds, taking in everything he had just heard.

"So, if your parents were actually murdered, that means mine were too."

His face got bright red. "I'm going to kill every last one of them. Slowly."

AFTER THEY WERE sure everything had calmed down in the hospital, they walked to the main road and hailed a cab. When they got to the bank, Shane waited in the cab while Dylan ran inside.

Dylan walked in and asked for the manager. A man came out of the back and asked what he could do for him. He was in his 40's, slightly overweight with a small beer belly and a greying goatee.

Dylan showed him the key for the safe deposit box and

told him it was his dad's box.

"Then why doesn't your dad come down and open it?" the bank manager asked in a condescending tone.

"My dad passed away a week ago," Dylan said with his best 'you've really hurt my feelings' voice.

The bank manager's face showed that he knew he'd just made a mistake. "I'm sorry young man, I didn't realize. Please forgive me. Without the proper paperwork and signatures, I just can't let you open up that box. Maybe you can get all of that together and I'll gladly open it for you."

Dylan knew this would probably be the case. He broke down in fake tears, begging and pleading with the man, asking him to make one exception.

"I know exactly what's in the box," said Dylan. "How would I know that if I wasn't telling the truth!? It's a manila envelope with a book inside it. It has all the proof I need to get my inheritance from my step mother who took everything from me! Go check! I swear I'm telling the truth!"

The bank manager hesitantly agreed and took the key from Dylan. Two minutes later the man came back, holding the manila envelope.

"Okay son. I'm not supposed to do this, but since you knew what was in the box, I'm assuming you are telling the truth. Normally I wouldn't just take your word for it, but I had the same thing happen when my dad died. So I'm going to let you have this."

"Thank you sir! Thank you! You don't know how much this means to me! I'll pay you back someday, I swear!"

"No need son. Just get that money back from your step mom. She doesn't deserve it."

Dylan turned around with a smile on his face, walked out of the bank, got in the cab and they were off to Loveland to meet up with Agent Larsen.

12

THE MEET

They pulled up to Lakeside Park at 7:00 pm and sat on a bench facing the lake. They had an hour to kill, so they discussed their time at The Denver Toy House and all the similarities of their lives. They hadn't realized when they first became friends how connected their lives had been. It was as if they were destined to meet each other.

It was 10 minutes to 8:00 pm, so they kept their eyes out for anyone that looked suspicious and for someone wearing sunglasses.

After about 5 minutes, they spotted a man in a suit and tie wearing sunglasses, looking around for something or someone.

"That's got to be him," said Dylan. "He's wearing sunglasses like I asked him to, and he looks like an FBI agent. What do you think?"

"Yeah, he definitely looks the part. Let's go talk to him and see if he's someone we can trust."

They casually strolled up to the man who had his back to them, looking in the opposite direction for someone.

"Agent Larsen?" asked Dylan.

The man in the sunglasses turned around. "Dylan and Shane, I take it? So you said you had some kind of proof of your innocence?"

Dylan handed him the envelope.

"Okay, I'll look at what's in this, but if you're lying, I'm taking you in right now."

Agent Larsen pulled the book out of the envelope and opened it to the first page. He stared at the book for several minutes, flipping the pages every now and then. After several minutes of skimming through, he looked up at them, eyes wide.

It was a detailed list of all things A.I.M.: every A.I.M. agent Waters knew about and where they were planted, details about The Denver Toy House and what they were doing to the kids there, and details about the New Hope Boys Home and the training and experiments with mind control that were being done. Everything about the agency was in that book.

"I know half of the people on this list! There are 3 in my office! Where'd you get this again?"

"I told you. Mr. Waters gave it to us before Mr. Mooney killed him. Do you believe us now?"

"Yeah, I do. We need to start making calls, so we can put a stop to this!"

Dylan shook his head and said, "No! That's not gonna work! Mr. Waters said that there are A.I.M. agents embedded everywhere. He said that it's just a list of the ones he is absolutely sure of. We need to be extremely cautious, because there are undoubtedly more agents he didn't know about. We need to do this ourselves. You need to round up people you trust, people not on that list, and you should use the code phrase I used to make sure you weren't an A.I.M. Agent. Mention Amy Mason from Colorado Springs. You can trust them if they don't react to the phrase. If we aren't careful about who we trust, A.I.M. will know we are coming and shut everything down before we are able to stop them. Or worse yet, we might be hunted down and killed before we can put an end to A.I.M. We need to take them by surprise."

"Okay kid, you're smarter than I gave you credit for. Where are you guys staying right now?"

"We've been living in a cabin up by Lake Granby. It's in the woods to the southeast of the lake."

Agent Larsen thought for a moment before he said, "Okay, so I'm going to take you to the cabin right now. Then I'll gather up some people I know and trust. We will be by the cabin in the next few days to go over our options. Sound good?"

They agreed that it was the best option. Agent Larsen drove them as close as he could, and they told him how to get to the cabin from where he dropped them off. He told them to sit tight, and he'd be back soon. They hiked back to the cabin, excited for the opportunity to get their revenge.

As Agent Larsen drove back from the mountain, his mind was going a mile a minute. It was hard to believe that there was actually an agency training young kids to become unknowing assassins, but he had seen the evidence with his own eyes. He couldn't believe that people he trusted, people he'd have over for weekend barbecues, were secret agents doing experiments on kids as young as 5 years old. His blood boiled at the thought of being lied to like that.

When he got home, he went through the book again and again. He was up all night making notes about who he thought he could trust, and the next day he began making calls using the code Dylan had told him to use. When he was done with all of his calls, he made a list of the people he could trust to help them.

There were three fellow FBI agents that had passed the code word test, and he knew all of them personally. He also called up his old friend from his time in the Marines, Brody Reeves. He also passed the test, although Larsen had no doubt that he would. He was a solid individual, and Larsen trusted him 100%.

Reeves retired from the Marines and started his own contracting company shortly after. He had asked Larsen if he'd like to leave the FBI and join him on his team, "to get away from the boring life of a desk jockey" as he put it, but Larsen turned him down. "I like being a boring desk jockey," he told him. "Less bullets." But Larsen knew his company would be perfect for this mission. They were well disciplined, well trained soldiers, and he knew Reeves wouldn't turn down THIS opportunity.

During his call to Reeves, he let Reeves know everything. He then suggested that Reeves should do an interrogation with each of his men, just in case they were A.I.M. Reeves assured him they were all trustworthy men, but he would question each one just to make sure.

After Larson had his list of people, he called everyone back and gave them the coordinates for where he had dropped off the boys. He told everyone to meet there at noon the next day. They would all hike to the cabin that the boys were staying in, and they would discuss their next moves.

13

BACK AT THE CABIN

After they were dropped off by Agent Larsen, Dylan and Shane started their hike back to the cabin. It was slow going due to Shane's injury, but they took their time and talked about the things to come.

"I hope Agent Larsen is able to find enough people," Shane said with a tinge of doubt in his voice. "I mean, we're going up against a whole agency of God knows how many people, and they are going to be extremely well trained."

"Yeah, but the good news is that they trained US too. Sure, we may not remember it, but it's in here somewhere," Dylan said, pointing to his head. "We just have to figure out how to get it out."

"Yeah, I guess you're right. But it's going to take some time. I still need to heal before I can even train at all."

"Yeah, we've got time though. I'll hopefully start training once Agent Larsen and whoever he's able to recruit get here. I'm going to tell him when he gets here that I want to make sure we do this correctly. Even if it takes a year of training, I want to make sure we are fully prepared for what we have to face.

"Also, I think we have the upper hand right now. Since we just had a run in with those A.I.M. agents, they probably think we've fled, probably out of the state. They most likely don't know that we've found an FBI contact or that we have the ability to plan out and launch an assault. They think we are just kids, and that we don't pose a threat. Let's make sure we can prove them wrong."

WHEN THEY ARRIVED BACK at the cabin, Shane laid down on the couch to rest, and Dylan went out to grab some wood for the wood stove. Dylan cooked up some venison for dinner, and they sat down to eat. They were extremely hungry because they hadn't had the time to eat all day.

Shane pulled off the wrapping on his leg, and they were both still in awe of how big the wound was. The doctor told Shane, while he was stitching him up, how lucky he had been. One more inch toward the inside of his leg, and the femoral artery would've been cut open. He wouldn't have even made it to the road, let alone the hospital.

Dylan helped him re-bandage the leg. They were extremely tired from the excitement of the day, and neither of them made it to their beds that night. They both passed out sitting up on the couch, and didn't move until they woke up the next morning.

The sun was shining through the cabin's front window when Dylan finally woke in the morning. He got up, made some breakfast and then woke up Shane. It was already 11:00 am. They were so tired they nearly slept through half the day.

"Hopefully Agent Larsen was able to get a group together. He said he'll be by in the next few days. We still need some more food, especially if we are going to have company. I'm going to go on a hunt. Will you be fine here by yourself?"

"I think I can manage...mom," said Shane with sarcasm in his voice.

"Very funny. I should be back in a few hours. Do you need me to grab you anything? Some soda, or chips or something?"

"Get outta here man! I'll be fine," Shane laughed, and then pointed at his leg. "Just watch out for mountain lions."

DYLAN WAS out for about an hour and a half when he finally got a kill. He took down a young buck from 40 yards with a perfectly placed shot. Hunting was now second nature to him. He butchered the deer with surgical precision, which had also become second nature, and headed back to the cabin with his haul.

On his way back, he heard a twig snap to his left in some underbrush, and he stopped dead in his tracks. He heard a low, steady growl coming from the bushes. About twenty feet ahead of him, a huge wolf slowly came out of the bushes, head down, audibly growling and it was blocking the path. Its eyes were locked onto Dylan's. Dylan slowly stepped backwards grabbing the bow and reached back to grab an arrow from the quiver, but there were none. He was so confident in his ability as a hunter that he had gotten into the habit of bringing just one arrow as a sort of challenge. He had forgotten the arrow in the meadow when he was butchering the deer. He laid the bow down slowly, and pulled out his hunting knife. He was going to have to take on this wolf with just a knife, or die trying.

Just then, the wolf took off towards him and leaped into

the air to try and grab Dylan by the throat. Dylan moved to his right to avoid the wolf's snapping jaws, and they both went down to the ground. The wolf landed on top, and Dylan had its neck in his left hand. The wolf was struggling to get to Dylan's neck as Dylan plunged the blade into its flank twice. The wolf howled in pain and backed off briefly, just enough for Dylan to plunge the knife into its neck. The wolf let out a disturbing gurgling sound and fell limp on top of Dylan. He quickly pushed the wolf off of him and got up, checking his body to see if any of the blood was his. None of it was. He had somehow just taken down a full grown wolf with just a knife, and he didn't have a scratch on him.

When he got to the cabin, he walked in the front door covered in blood, and Shane's jaw dropped.

"What the hell happened! Are you ok!?"

Dylan stood there silently and finally said, "Yeah, I'm fine. I was just attacked by a wolf, and I killed it. With a knife."

"Wait, what? You killed a WOLF with a knife!? No way man!"

"Yeah, it's about a quarter mile down the path to the meadow. I need to take a shower and rest for a little while. Can you put away the deer meat I got?"

"Yeah, sure man, no prob. Take all the time you need. You sure you're okay?"

Dylan nodded his head and turned toward the bathroom. He took a shower, then laid down to try and calm down from all the adrenaline that was still coursing through his veins. He was fast asleep after a few minutes.

AGENT LARSEN PULLED up to the spot where he had dropped off the boys two days prior, and there were several other cars all parked together. He got out of his car and walked up to the group of men standing in a circle talking. His friend, Brody Reeves, turned around.

"Sam Larsen! How you doing man? It's been too long! I think everyone is here. This is my team: Levitt, Snyder, Jackson and Morris. They are completely trustworthy, and they are all in a hundred percent."

Larsen shook each of their hands, and gave Reeves a hug.

"Good to see you bud! I'm really glad you could make it. I wasn't sure you'd come."

"Of course I would Sam! You're like a brother to me. Anything you need, me and my men are here for you."

"Glad to hear that Brody. Well, I see you've met my fellow FBI agents. Cowden, Lawsen, Wilson, thanks for coming out. You guys are some of the only people I can trust right now. Let's go ahead to the cabin. I'll introduce you to the kids, and I'll fill everyone in on what's going on."

They all grabbed their gear and made their way down the path towards the cabin.

"HERE THEY ARE!" Dylan said excitedly.

He walked over to the front door and opened it to greet Agent Larsen and the others.

"Agent Larsen! You made it! I see you were able to gather some men. Come on in. There's some venison steaks if anyone's hungry."

Reeves leaned over to Agent Larsen and whispered, "Man, when you said we would be helping kids out, I assumed you meant kids as in their lower twenties. I didn't know you meant ACTUAL kids. What are they? Fourteen, fifteen?"

"Actually, we're eighteen," Dylan said. "But I don't see why that matters. We aren't helpless little kids. We've been trained by A.I.M., although it's still mostly hidden in our subconscious. Some of it has come to the surface. I just killed a wolf yesterday with just a hunting knife when it attacked me. Have you ever done that?"

Reeve's face got red. He didn't realize Dylan could hear him. "I didn't mean it like that kid. I just meant...wait, you said you killed a wolf with your knife!?"

"That's right. It's about a quarter mile down the path behind the cabin, unless another animal dragged it away already. Feel free to check if you don't believe me."

"No, I believe you kid. Maybe I misjudged you. Let's head inside and talk about this A.I.M. group. I'm curious to hear what this is all about."

Dylan led the men inside, and they introduced themselves. Afterwards, they all took seats around the living room in a large circle. Agent Larsen was the first to speak.

"Okay gentlemen, now that we've all been acquainted, let's get down to business. As you all know, I've picked all of you for this mission because you are the only people I can truly trust right now. Dylan and Shane here were the ones who brought everything we are about to discuss to my attention. There is a secret agency that is recruiting and training kids as young as 5 years old to become sleeper assassins for them. They have agents planted in almost every law enforcement agency in Colorado, and probably the whole country."

He turned towards the boys. "Dylan, Shane, you guys are the ones who brought this to my attention and you were a part of the program. Do you guys want to take it from here?"

Dylan and Shane then went on to explain how they had

been recruited by A.I.M. when they were 6, how A.I.M. killed their parents, their life at the boys home, how they escaped and were framed for the murder of Mr. Waters, and how they had come to find this cabin. Dylan explained that they were finding out skills they never knew they had, which were part of their training at the boys home. When they were finished with their story, all the men looked at each other, amazed at what they had heard.

Reeves stood up and said, "Well I'm in! These guys can't get away with this! My men and I will do whatever it takes. So, when are we gonna do this? We can plan it out right now and take down these sons of bitches!"

"We can't do it yet," said Dylan. "I was going to bring that up earlier. We need to take our time with this. A.I.M. knows what they are doing. We can't just go in there without making damn sure we are ready for whatever they can throw our way. Plus, Shane's leg needs to heal, and we both need more training. We need to see what we are capable of.

"My plan was for Agent Larsen and the other agents to go back to their normal routine, but do some surveillance on the main A.I.M. building in Colorado Springs and also at the New Hope Boys Home. Mr. Reeves, you and your men can go back down tonight and make whatever arrangements you need and then you can come back up here and train me and Shane. Once we are ready, we can all meet up again and plan out our attack."

"Well son," Reeves said, impressed. "You're thorough, I'll give you that. I think it's a great plan. My men and I will head down the mountain to grab some equipment, and we will be back up here in a day or two."

"Dylan, Shane," said Larsen. "We are all with you on this. My fellow agents and I will keep an eye on those two locations, and we will keep in touch. When you feel that you're

ready, we can all meet at an FBI safehouse in Colorado
Springs to make the final preparations. If all goes as planned,
we can take out the whole operation and you two will get
your justice."

Everyone said their goodbyes. After all the men left,
Dylan and Shane sat around talking excitedly about the possibility of getting the revenge they'd been dreaming about for
the last few years.

14

TRAINING BEGINS

Two days later Reeves and his men arrived back at the cabin. They were greeted at the door by Dylan and Shane. After they all said their hellos, they took seats in a circle in the living room to go over what their training would entail.

"Okay boys, we are going to be putting you through the wringer. We are going to do your training in three phases. The first phase is getting your scrawny asses in shape. Build some muscle on those bones. Shane, you can join in on this portion of the training, but we can go easy on you until your leg fully heals. I hope you're ready to get your asses kicked.

"After we get you into shape, the second phase will be weapons training. We will be hiking deep into the woods where no one will hear us. We brought plenty of non-lethal training rounds for the war games we will be having, and we will be teaching you different war tactics, including close quarters combat. We will be teaching you how to sneak up on your enemies with stealth for silent kills. By the end of this phase, you will be proficient killing machines.

"The last phase, which I think will be your favorite, is

demolitions. We need to do this last because it will definitely draw attention to us, and we will need to be heading out of here shortly after. We most likely won't be using explosives on the mission because we will be in close quarters, but you never know. Plus, it's just fun to blow stuff to hell. Any questions?"

"How long is all this going to take?" Dylan asked.

"Well, that all depends on you two. I will be doing physical training with you boys until Shane is all healed and ready to go. My men will be going out and scouting for training areas, and also doing some training themselves while they are out there. Once both of you are in shape, which could take several months, we will start on your combat training. When you two prove to be ready for the mission, I'll contact Agent Larsen, we will blow some stuff up, and then head to Colorado Springs to rendezvous with the rest of the team and come up with our plan of attack."

"Okay," Dylan said. "Like I said before, I don't want to rush things. I want everything to be perfect. So please don't say we are ready if you THINK we are ready. I want you to KNOW we are ready."

"I wouldn't have it any other way. We are all part of a team, and we need to trust each other with our lives. The tough reality is that some of us might not make it through this. If we train you boys correctly, we should all be able to make it through this without a scratch."

"Okay, that sounds good," Dylan said with an air of satisfaction. "Let's get to it then."

FOR THE FIRST two months together, while Shane's thigh healed, Reeves put Dylan through a light physical training program to get his strength up for the real training that was to come. While Dylan and Reeves did their training outside, Shane would stay in the cabin doing push ups and sit ups and anything else that wouldn't put much stress on his leg. Shane joined them for some heavier training once his leg was healed enough. They went on daily hikes into the mountains, adding a half mile every two days. They dug holes around the cabin, three feet in diameter, until it was just above their head. Then climbed out and filled them back in, only to do it over again a few days later.

If Dylan and Shane were ever tired or wanted to give up, they never showed it. They did every exercise, every chore and they did it all without question. Reeves was extremely impressed with their tenacity and willingness to take on what-ever he threw at them.

Over those first months, the boys transformed from typical looking skinny 17 year old kids, to toned, muscular young men. Shane's thigh was now about 90 percent healed and after weeks of Shane insisting he was perfectly fine to start the full blown training, Reeves decided Shane's leg was good to go.

The first exercise Reeves had for them was to hike 20 miles with full gear into the deep forest to a gorge his men had found for their weapons training. There were human shaped targets lined up at various distances, and a long folding table with various firearms laid out on it. There were 9mm's, .45's, AK-47's, MP-5's, SMG's and a .50 caliber BMG.

"Okay boys," said Reeves. "Time for some weapons train-ing. Have either of you ever used a firearm before?"

"We've used the rifle we found in the cabin to hunt a few times, but we didn't want to bring any attention to ourselves, so we've mostly used the bow and arrow," said Dylan.

"Okay, so you have a basic idea of how it feels to shoot a gun. We will start you off shooting the 9mm's to gage where you're at with your accuracy, and then we will move up accordingly until you are deadly accurate with every gun.

"Dylan, why don't you go ahead and step up to the table, grab the 9mm and take aim at the nearest target."

Dylan stepped up to the table, picked up the gun and cocked it. He raised the gun and set the sights on the nearest target, about 20 feet away.

"Okay Dylan, now aim at the center mass, right in the center of the chest, take a deep brea..."

Two shots rang out in quick succession, and Reeves looked down range at the target. One shot was placed directly in center mass, and as an unexpected bonus, one directly in the center of the forehead.

"Okay then, I can see you're a little more proficient than I gave you credit for Dylan. Shane, why don't you go ahead and step up, and we can see where you're at."

Shane approached the table, picked up the 9mm, and held it out in front of him. He took aim at the closest target and put two shots within an inch of either of Dylan's shots. And to show up his friend, put a third shot directly in center mass of the target that was 40 feet away.

"Well then, I can see both of you can shoot a handgun at a decent distance. How did you get so accurate without practice?"

"Well, we can't be positive," said Shane, "but we are pretty sure it's from the training we had at the Boys Home. We were under hypnosis, so it's probably buried in our subconscious somewhere. It felt like second nature just now when I pulled the trigger. I didn't even have to think about it."

Reeves laughed. "Well, then it's going to be a lot easier to train you than I thought. Let's go ahead and go down the line of the guns I have here and see how you do on longer distance shots. We will save the .50 Cal for last and see how you do with extreme distance."

They spent the rest of the day shooting, and they did not lose accuracy with any of the guns. Neither of the boys missed their targets that day, no matter how far. Reeves was seriously impressed by their shooting skills. Towards the end of the day, he had one of his men hike up to a ridge a half mile away and place a few targets. Once the targets were in place, and after a few short lessons on wind velocity, air density, and bullet trajectory, the boys took turns hitting the targets one by one.

When they were done for the day, the team set up camp and got ready for a dinner of venison cooked over an open flame. After dinner, they sat around the campfire, recalling the day.

"You boys seriously impressed me today. I've seen soldiers train for years and still not be as accurate as you two. I think we will continue with weapons training for another day or two just to make sure you are a hundred percent ready, and then in a few days we will split into two teams and we can play out several scenarios with non-lethal rounds. Now let's relax around this fire and have some well deserved rest."

OVER THE NEXT few days they continued the firearms training, not that they needed it. They hit every target, every time. They were definitely the most proficient shooters Reeves had ever seen. After the second day, he told them it was time for the war games. They were excited to see how they would do.

Reeves had his second best soldier, Snyder, take Dylan and Shane out deep into the woods. Their goal, with the help of Snyder, was to find the camp that Reeves and the other men set up, and to ultimately "take out" Reeves with either a non lethal round, or with a blade if they could get close enough.

The rules were easy: take out Reeves. That was it. If they couldn't find him, or were "killed" by one of Reeves' men, they would have to return back to their base and try again the next day after Reeves and his men had a chance to move their base. If they were able to take out Reeves several times without getting taken out themselves, they would prove themselves ready and they could start the mission.

It didn't take long for them to take out Reeves. Their first try was all it took. The first day, Snyder taught them how to track by showing them what to look and listen for. He taught them to use all of their senses to find clues and signs of where the target could be. After three hours, Dylan stopped his teammates; he had caught a mild whiff of burning tobacco. They silently moved towards the smell, following the light breeze and found Morris smoking a cigarette by himself.

Dylan signaled to Shane and Snyder that he would flank Morris, and they should make a noise to draw Morris' attention when he gives the signal. Dylan would then sneak up behind Morris, and take him out with a blade. It worked perfectly.

They found Reeves' camp ten minutes later. Shane came up with the plan this time. He and Snyder would flank the left and right purposely drawing Levitt and Jackson to them, leaving Reeves unprotected. Dylan would then sneak up behind him, and take him out.

The first part of the plan worked perfectly. Shane and Snyder were able to lure Levitt and Jackson to them, and took them out easily. Dylan was just about to take out Reeves from behind, when he stepped on a twig, alerting Reeves to his presence. Reeves turned around reaching for his sidearm, but it was too late. Dylan had his knife to his neck already. Their team won the first round.

After three weeks, Dylan and Shane were able to sneak up and take out Reeves enough times that it was undeniable. They were ready.

REEVES PULLED up to a payphone in Granby and made a call to Agent Larsen. The phone rang for quite a while and just as Reeves was about to hang up, Larsen picked up the phone.

"This is Agent Larsen."

"Hey Larsen, it's Reeves. It took way less time than I originally thought, but it's time. I've been putting them through the paces, and they are some of the best soldiers I've ever seen. I think we might actually be able to pull it off."

"Good to hear Brody. Go ahead and pack up there and head to our safehouse in Colorado Springs. It's at 805 South Logan Avenue. It's right across the street from the park at Prospect Lake. Once you get here, we can go over our plans and prepare for the mission. So just to be sure, you are ABSOLUTELY positive they are ready for this mission? I can't have the deaths of these boys on my conscience because they weren't totally ready."

"I'm sure Sam. I'd worry more about us not being ready, to be honest. These kids have impressed me to no end. I'll go ahead and head back to the cabin, and we will make preparations to head to Colorado Springs. We should be there in the next day or two. See you soon."

REEVES ARRIVED BACK at the cabin and gathered the team for a meeting. They all sat around the cabin's living room eagerly awaiting the news of Reeves' call to Larsen.

"Ok men," said Reeves, looking directly at Dylan and Shane, acknowledging that they were men now. "I just talked to Agent Larsen and let him know we are ready for this mission. We are going to head to Colorado Springs, and meet up with Larsen and his fellow FBI agents at their safehouse, where we will be going over the plan for the mission. But first, after we pack up all our gear, I promised you we'd be blowing some stuff up.

"I thought, since you boys won't be coming back up here to hide after this mission, we'd blow this cabin to hell as a symbolic gesture. You know, to show yourselves you no longer have to hide up here. That you are ready to take on A.I.M. and put them down once and for all. What do you think?"

"Hell yes!" said Shane.

"Absolutely!" Dylan agreed. "We've had some good times up here, but we've also been up here hiding like scared rabbits. I don't want to hide anymore. I want our revenge."

They packed up all the gear and planted C-4 all around the cabin. They all loaded into the van, and Reeves handed Dylan the detonator as they drove away.

"The honor is all yours. Pull that trigger and your path to revenge will be set in motion."

Dylan looked at Shane, and Shane looked back at him and gave him a nod. Dylan closed his eyes, took a deep breath and pulled the trigger. With an enormous explosion, their destiny was now set.

15

THE SAFEHOUSE

The van pulled up to an unassuming one story house with an unkempt, small front yard. It was across the street from Prospect Lake, a small man made body of water that was more like a large pond, on the corner of Logan Avenue and Prospect Lake Drive in Colorado Springs. Dylan could understand why the FBI would choose it as a safehouse. No one would ever expect there were Federal Agents staying there. They'd be more inclined to feel sorry for the poor family that lived in the house.

"Okay guys stay in the van," said Reeves.

He walked up to the front door and pushed the doorbell. A few seconds later, Agent Larsen answered the door.

"Brody! Great to see you. Glad you guys are here. Go ahead and pull the van around to the side of the house, and you guys can unload your gear and get settled in."

Reeves pulled the van along the side of the house, and they unloaded their gear, taking care to look out for nosy neighbors. Once they had the van completely unloaded, they all headed into the house. The house looked much nicer on the inside than on the outside. There was a large living room, three large bedrooms with two bunk beds in each room, and a nice kitchen that was fully stocked. After everyone was in, Agent Larsen directed them to head down the stairway that was normally hidden behind the kitchen pantry. Then he followed behind them and closed the false door behind him. The basement was a large control center full of computer equipment, a weapons cache, and all the intelligence Larsen and the other agents had been collecting on A.I.M.

"Okay everyone, take a seat. First of all, welcome to Colorado Springs. I hope you had a nice ride in. Dylan and Shane, Reeves tells me you two are more than ready. I'm very pleased to hear that because it's going to be a tough mission. I and my fellow agents have all taken a leave of absence. As far as the Bureau knows, we are all on vacation in Hawaii.

"In our spare time we've been doing some surveillance on the A.I.M. Facility at the ABC Supply building, the New Hope Boys Home and also The Denver Toy House, looking for anything that might help us with the mission. We've spent the last couple days coming up with a plan of attack."

Larsen wheeled over a large whiteboard that had surveillance photos taped to it with writing all over the board.

"We've been surveilling three main subjects. If we can take out these three men, I believe we can take down A.I.M. for good, and rescue any kids they have in their custody.

"Our main target is the leader of A.I.M and The Denver Toy House, Mr. Bryant, a.k.a. Dante Sellers. He started out at the FBI and was then recruited by the CIA in 1972. Shortly after that, his paper trail abruptly ends and we don't know much from there. We assume he was absorbed into one of the CIA's shadow programs, most likely MKUltra due to the nature of what he's been doing with kids like you. At some point, officially 1975, but likely a while after that, MKUltra dissolved and our best guess is he formed A.I.M. at this time and continued his work.

"The second subject is the head of The New Hope Boys Home and Seller's right hand man, one Phillip Kane. He joined the Marines at 18 and transferred to the Navy to become a Navy SEAL at the age of 22. He was discharged after an incident where a civilian was killed in El Salvador. There was no proof, but he was thought to have killed the civilian over a poker game. It was investigated but they found no proof it was Kane, and the Marines let him go with an Other Than Honorable discharge. He worked various security jobs until settling as the head of New Hope in 1995.

"Which leads us to our last subject, Robin Mooney. Also a Marine, but never made it to special forces. Did his four years and got out with an Honorable Discharge. Tried to join the Sheriff's Department, but couldn't pass the Psychological Test. He showed signs of narcissism, a lack of empathy, and a lack of remorse or guilt to name a few. He was hired on to New Hope in 1997. Any questions so far?"

Dylan raised his hand. "Mooney's first name is Robin? Makes sense." He and Shane started laughing to themselves.

"Well, as there are no SERIOUS questions, I'll move on. We've found out that there isn't any armed security at The Denver Toy House, probably because they don't want to chance any parents seeing armed personnel around the building. Same goes with New Hope. So those will be our lower priority targets. However, we will be doing further surveillance on both to ensure we can take them over when it's time.

"Over the next week or so, we agents will be watching all three buildings looking for weak spots and anything else that can help us. I've made an appointment as a small business owner looking for office supplies, so I'll be able to check out the inside of the ABC Supply building. Dylan and Shane, you can join the surveillance on the other two buildings, so you can point out things you know about the operations we may not know about. We can't take too many chances with you boys being spotted, so you can only go once or twice, and only at night. That's all I have for now. I'm sure you men would like some rest, so I'll show you to your rooms."

DYLAN AND SHANE sat in the back seat of the Honda Civic, down the street from the New Hope Boys Home. It was a clear, beautiful moonlit night, and they were on their first official stakeout. Reeves and Levitt were in the front seat, and Reeves turned in his seat to look back at the boys.

"Okay guys. This can get pretty boring, so hold onto your seats. Just keep an eye out and if you see anyone you recognize or if you have any input that could be helpful, just let us know. Otherwise, it's just a whole lot of sitting around."

"Well," said Dylan. "I do have one suggestion. If we pull the car up the street a little, we can have a view of the main building AND the education building."

"See. You're being helpful already!"

Reeves started the car, pulled around the block, and parked in the spot Dylan had pointed out. He put the car in park, and turned back to Dylan and Shane.

"So, any info on the two buildings? Entrances? Exits? Any hidden rooms that you know of?" asked Levitt.

"The main building has two entrances," said Shane. "One in front and one in back. There are three floors. The bottom floor has the cafeteria, recreation room and all the staff offices. The two top floors are living quarters for the kids.

There are about sixteen rooms total, eight each floor, with room for two boys in each room.

"Then the education building also has two entrances. The building has two floors, with six classrooms on either floor. Nothing special."

Dylan spoke up, "What about what Mr. Waters told us?" He turned towards Reeves. "When he was helping us escape, he told us that they were doing experiments on us boys in a secret bunker underneath the education building. He said there was an entrance under a tarp on the east side of the building. I think that's where we were trained also."

"That's perfect you two. Very helpful stuff. I think when the time comes, we will have no problem taking this operation down. There are no armed personnel I've seen. Now that we know about the secret bunker and that they possibly have weapons down there, we can secure that first. Now, let's keep our eyes open for any comings or goings."

A FEW HOURS LATER, Shane broke the silence. "Hey!" he said, nudging Dylan. "Is that Kane? Back there, coming out of the education building?"

Dylan grabbed the binoculars Reeves had given him from off the seat, and put them up to his eyes.

"Yup. That's him. I can recognize those beady eyes anywhere. It looks like he's heading out of the side gate. Now he's getting in a car. Should we follow him? He's probably our best link to finding anything else out."

"Yeah, good idea Dylan. Let's see where he goes. It's been pretty quiet here, and he's the man in charge. Let's see where this takes us. He's coming this way. You two duck down, so he doesn't see you."

The boys laid down in the back seat, and Kane passed by a few seconds later. Reeves started the car and pulled out, keeping a reasonable distance so he wouldn't alert Kane to their presence. They followed him through the streets of Boulder to Highway 36 and into Denver. He pulled into the parking lot of The Denver Toy House, and parked his car. Reeves parked on the street half a block down, and turned off the car.

They watched through binoculars as a man walked out of the front entrance. They all recognized him from the white-board at the safehouse. It was Dante Sellers. He walked up to Kane, who was standing outside of his car. They had a conversation for several minutes, then Sellers handed Kane a manilla envelope and turned to walk back towards the building.

"I wish we could've heard what they were talking about," said Dylan. "It could've been something important."

"Well, let's just follow Kane and see where he goes from here," said Reeves.

Kane pulled out of the parking lot, and Reeves followed him. They drove through Denver and got onto the I25. They got off in Colorado Springs, and they followed him to the ABC Supply building. Kane got out of his car and went inside.

"Well," said Reeves. "I guess this is as far as we go. We obviously can't follow him in there, and it's late. Let's head back to the safehouse and brief Larsen on what we got tonight."

Reeves started up the car and turned it around. They headed back to the safehouse, where Larsen was eagerly waiting to hear what they had found out during their stakeout.

"So," said Larsen with a look of curiosity in his eyes. "What did you guys find out tonight?"

"Well, Dylan and Shane gave us some good intel on the Boys Home while we were there," said Reeves. "As we were talking about it, Shane noticed Kane walking out of one of the buildings. We followed him to The Denver Toy House, where he met up with none other than Dante Sellers. They had a small conversation and when they were done, Sellers gave Kane a package. We again followed Kane, this time all the way back here where he stopped at ABC Supply and went inside. That's when we came back here. It's not much, but we do know for sure now that they are communicating between all three facilities. All in all, I think it was a great night."

"Good to hear. I'm glad you two could help out. Reeves, go ahead and add any intel you learned to the board downstairs. Boys, let's grab a snack before you two settle down for the night. I've got a few questions for you."

Reeves headed down to the basement, and Dylan and Shane followed Larsen into the kitchen. Larsen grabbed some things out of the refrigerator and began making them some turkey sandwiches. As he was making the food, he asked them about the Boys Home.

"So, Reeves said you had some intel on the Boys Home. I just want to make sure you know these things for sure. How did you come upon this intel? I want to make sure we aren't going to run into a trap, or have the intel be bad and screw up our plans."

"The only thing we don't know for sure is about the bunker under the education building. We've apparently been in it, but neither of us remember it," said Dylan. "We were told by Mr. Waters right before he helped us escape. He died helping us get out, so I'm pretty sure we can trust what he told us. I want to get revenge for myself and Shane, but also for Waters. It's the least we can do for him."

"Okay, I just had to make sure. Don't you worry though. I'm confident we will come through victorious. Mr. Waters will get the retribution he deserves. Good job tonight boys. We are getting closer to mission time. Just a few more intel gathering missions and we will be ready to go. Finish up those sandwiches, and get some sleep. I'll see you two in the morning."

Dylan and Shane sat quietly eating their sandwiches, contemplating how close they were to finally getting their well deserved closure.

16

THE FINAL STAKEOUT

A few weeks had gone by since that first stakeout, and the team had gathered almost all of the intel they needed. Larsen wanted to do one last trip to the ABC Supply building to make sure all of their intel on shift changes and how many go in or out during the day and night was correct.

"Okay guys, we will do this last mission in shifts starting with Reeves and Dylan from 6:00 to 11:00 in the morning, Cowden and Snyder from 11:00 till 4:00, Lawson and Levitt from 4:00 till 9:00, Wilson and Jackson from 9:00 to 2:00 in the morning, and finally Shane and Morris from 2:00 to 6:00 am. That way we have eyes on the building for a full 24 hours."

Shane groaned. "Why do I have to do the early morning shift? A handsome guy like me needs his beauty sleep you know!"

"I picked the shifts at random from a hat Shane. Sorry for your luck. You can get your 'beauty' rest in the afternoon. Anyone ELSE have a problem with their shift? No? Okay, great. We will start tomorrow morning."

Shane walked over to Dylan and asked, "Hey buddy.

How'd you like to have the shorter four hour shift? I'd totally trade with you if you wanted. It'd be no trouble at all!"

"Not a chance Shane. Nice try though. It's not like mine is great either. I have to get up at like 5:00 tomorrow morning. Look, this is the last thing we have to do before the mission. We are so close to shutting down A.I.M. for good. We need to do this for Waters. He helped us, and it cost him his life. This is the least we can do."

"Yeah, I guess you're right. But I still don't like it. So you're absolutely SURE you don't want to trade with me?"

Dylan rolled his eyes. "I'm sure Shane. Quit asking. No one is going to want to trade, and I don't see Morris going around asking to trade. Suck it up buttercup."

Shane turned around and walked away, shoulders hunched, and went to his bed to quietly mope to himself.

SHANE'S ALARM went off at 1:00 am, and he woke with a groan. He got up out of bed and walked to the kitchen to grab a bite to eat before his shift. After he ate he took a quick shower, keeping it on cold to fully wake himself up. He sat in the living room for a few minutes before Morris came in and greeted him.

"Morning Shane. You ready? Just a few hours and we can hit the hay again. I was talking with Larsen earlier, and he said it's been pretty quiet at ABC all day. Just the normal traffic we've been seeing."

"Yeah, that's what Dylan told me this morning when he got back from his shift. I made a big thermos of coffee for us, so hopefully that'll keep us awake."

"Awesome. I definitely need some coffee. Let's go ahead and head over so we can take over for Wilson and

Jackson. I'm sure they are more than ready to get back and sleep."

They got in the car and drove to ABC. Morris pulled up behind Wilson and Jackson and got out of the car. He walked up to their car and tapped on the window.

"Hey guys. Any excitement tonight?"

Wilson closed his eyes and made a fake snoring sound.

"No. Super quiet so far. We haven't seen one person all night. You guys should have an exciting night. I hope you guys loaded up on coffee."

"Of course we did. Well, you two can head back and get some sleep. Shane and I have it from here. See you in a few hours."

Morris turned around and walked back to his car as Wilson and Jackson drove away. He opened the door and sat back down in the driver's seat.

"They said it's been quiet since 11:00. No one has gone in or out. So let's have a cup of coffee, put on some music and just keep our eyes open. In four hours, we can go home and sleep."

SHANE AWOKE to the sound of a struggle. He didn't remember falling asleep, but apparently he did. He looked over to see Morris just outside of the car fighting with another man. He was instantly awake. He jumped out of the car and ran over to help Morris. Just as he was about to hit the attacker, he saw another man in his periphery bearing down on him. He tried to turn to defend himself, but it was too late. The man hit him, and he went down. He pushed himself back up, but the man's foot made contact with his face and the lights went out.

Morris was bleeding on the ground as the two men picked

up Shane to bring him inside the building. Morris tried to get up to help him but couldn't seem to find the strength. He pulled up his shirt and saw a huge gash in his stomach. At some point in the melee he had been stabbed. He mustered up any last bit of power he had and climbed back into the car. He picked up his radio and pushed down the button.

"Come in! Come in! Anybody at the safehouse, do you read me!"

"This is Larsen. I read you loud and clear."

"We've been ambushed! I've been stabbed and they took Shane! I'm heading back to the safehouse. Get the medical kit out. I'll be there in a few minutes!"

Morris started the car and drove as fast as he could back to the safehouse.

He pulled up to the house, blaring the horn. Larsen, Reeves and Levitt were the first people out of the house. They got to the car, pulled Morris out and quickly carried him inside.

"What happened Morris!" yelled Larsen. "What happened to Shane?!"

"We were sitting in the car, and Shane had fallen asleep. There wasn't anything going on, so I figured I'd just let him sleep. Then, what I thought was a homeless man pushing a shopping cart passed by the car."

He winced in pain as Reeves was working on him trying to stop the bleeding. "I don't feel so good Larsen. I don't wanna go out like this man!"

"You'll be fine Morris," Larsen lied. "Keep going. What happened with the homeless man?"

"He asked for some change, and I told him I didn't have anything. He started to make a bunch of noise and I didn't want to draw any attention to us, so I got out of the vehicle to get him to shut up. As I got out of the vehicle, he slammed the door against me. I was able to get out and defend myself. I noticed Shane getting out of the passenger side to help me, and that's when another man ambushed him. I was stabbed sometime in the course of the fight and couldn't help him. They took him inside of ABC. I'm telling you Larsen, I'm not feeling so go..."

Morris had lost consciousness. Reeves checked his pulse. There wasn't one. He quickly started doing chest compressions, trying to bring him back. After a few minutes, he finally stopped. Morris was dead.

SHANE SLOWLY CAME TO, still dazed from being knocked unconscious. When his mind finally cleared, he realized he was strapped to a chair in a drab, featureless room. He struggled to break free, but quickly realized his bonds were too tight to escape from. His head was pounding from the blow he received. The doorknob to the room jiggled briefly as someone was unlocking it, and Mr. Kane walked into the room.

"Ahh, Shane. You're awake! It's been too long. I was afraid I'd never see you again. Last time we saw each other, we left on such bad terms. You left without saying goodbye. That really hurt my feelings."

"Well, now that you're back, we can catch up. We know that you've been planning on trying to stop our organization with the help of some agents."

Shane's eyes widened. *They knew about that? How could they possibly know?*

"Yeah, we have people everywhere Shane. We lost track of you two for a while, but when some of our agents caught sight of you at the hospital in Boulder, we've been watching you ever since, biding our time. We would've just killed you right away, but you two were our best candidates in quite a long time. So we will forgive you for the whole running away thing."

"We've got you, and now we will just wait for your 'team' to show up to rescue you. Then we will have Dylan too. We have more than enough man power here to take out a few agents and a kid. Once we have both of you back, we will finish your training and you'll never even remember these last few years. It'll be like they never even happened."

Shane stared at Kane for a few long seconds, then he broke the silence.

"Congratulations Kane. You got me. But I seriously think you're underestimating our chances. But good luck with all that."

"See, that's where you're wrong Shane. It's YOU who's underestimating US. We have the upper hand here. We know everything about you, we outnumber you, and we have better training than you. Your little rag tag group of friends don't stand a chance."

"Well, I guess we'll just have to wait and see about that, asshole. I'm going to love watching you die. I want to be looking into your eyes as you slip into hell."

17

REVENGE

The safehouse was in chaos after Morris took his last breath. Down in the bunker, everyone was running around, grabbing weapons and all were eager to get revenge for Morris' death. Through all the mayhem, Larsen whistled as loud as he could to get the attention of everyone in the house.

"Listen up everyone! I know that you're mad and you want to get them back for Morris. But that's exactly what they want. They want us worked up and unorganized. They want us running in, guns blazing, without a real plan. We need to make a plan, and it's going to have to be good. We no longer have the advantage of surprise because they know we are coming.

"Let's all catch our breath and figure this out. We still have a good shot at saving Shane. Morris said he was still alive when they took him. My guess is they want him for bait. They are going to try and take Dylan alive, so they can still use him as an assassin. Now, I have an idea of what might work, but seeing as we are all on the same team you can all speak up if you see something wrong with what I think we should do."

Larsen walked over to grab the whiteboard and rolled it over. There was a large satellite image of the area on it, covering the area from the safehouse to the ABC Supply Company building. As he began talking again, he used a pen to highlight the areas he was discussing.

"First, we will all travel down Las Animas on foot towards ABC. It's early in the morning, so the streets will be empty. We still need to stay vigilant and stick to the shadows as much as possible.

"Once we get to Cascade Avenue, here," Larsen pointed to the map, "we will split into three teams. Team Alpha, which will be Cowden, Wilson and myself, Team Bravo will be Dylan, Levitt and Jackson, and Team Charlie will be Reeves, Lawsen and Synder.

"After we split up, Team Bravo will move into a position covering the south side of the building, Charlie will cover the north side, and Alpha will cover the front of the building. Once we are in position, we will decide our plan of action to get into the building. We may have men waiting for us or some kind of trap.

"Once we get into the main building, there is a main hallway with a total of four offices connected to it, which we will have to clear, before heading onto the factory floor. We will make our way to the northwest corner of the building, where the door to the bunker is located. From there, we will be winging it as we have no intel on the bunker. Any questions or suggestions?"

Everyone seemed to be on board with the plan of attack, so Larsen put the cap back on the pen, rolled the board back and turned towards the men.

"Okay then! Everyone grab your gear, and we will head

out in fifteen!"

IT WAS four in the morning and they were making their way down Las Animas Street on foot, constantly watching for any enemies or police patrolling the neighborhood. Anytime there was a car in sight, which wasn't very often considering the time, they would take cover behind any parked cars or in the shadows.

When they got to Cascade Avenue, two blocks away from the ABC Supply Company, Larsen silently motioned for the nine men to break into the groups of three they had chosen. Team Bravo went left down Cascade, Team Charlie went right, and Team Alpha continued down Las Animas.

Dylan, Levitt and Jackson found a spot on the corner of Sierra Nevada and Fountain, in some bushes about 500 feet away from the southeast corner of the building. Dylan laid down in the prone position and put his eye to the scope. He scanned the area looking for any A.I.M. agents waiting for them. He spotted some men on the roof.

"This is Team Bravo. We're in position. I've got an eye on two sniper teams, four men total. One team is on the southeast corner nearest our position. The other team is dead center of the building looking towards Sierra Nevada. There are no men on the ground that I can see. I can't see the other side of the building. Team Charlie, do you have eyes on that side of the building yet? Over."

A few seconds passed and Reeves' voice came over the radio. "This is Team Charlie. We are also in position. I have sight on a third sniper team on the north side of the building. I have a perfect view of the front of the building. The lights are out, so we will need our night vision when we breach the building. There are no other men besides the three teams on the roof. Over."

"This is Team Alpha." It was Larsen's voice. "I see all three teams on the roof now. Before we take our shots, Levitt, see if you can get eyes on the west side of the building. I want to make sure there's no one else on the roof. Over."

"10-4 Charlie. Give me a few minutes."

Levitt took off to check out the backside of the building. Two minutes later, his voice came through the radio. "This is Levitt. I've checked the west side and there are no other teams on the roof. I'm coming up behind Bravo now."

"This is Team Bravo. Levitt is back in position. I've got my sights on the shooter nearest me. Just say the word Alpha. Over."

"Okay, all three of us are going to have to take simultaneous shots, reload and take our second shots right away. When you have a clear shot, give me a 'ready.' I will count down from five, and we shoot on one. Are we clear?"

"10-4, Team Bravo is ready."

"Team Charlie, ready."

" Okay boys. Pull your triggers in five... four... three... two..."

In less than one second, every shot hit its mark and all six men on the roof went down. The three teams sat patiently for several minutes, making sure no one else was up there. Once they knew it was all clear, Larsen spoke to everyone over the radio.

"Good shots boys. Phase One is complete. Now on to Phase Two. Everyone, switch to your night vision goggles. Now once we breach the front doors, there may or may not be men waiting for us. If there are, we will have a fire fight to deal with. We've all had training with the military, and Dylan, well, you should be more than fine.

"Team Bravo, you three approach from the south side of the building, and Charlie will approach from the north. We will all convene at the front door, and then we can breach. Move out."

Dylan and his team crossed the street and moved in on the south side of the building, taking cover behind whatever they could and keeping an eye out for any enemies. They got to the south east corner of the building and got into cover.

When they saw Larsen and his team approach from the front, they turned the corner towards the front entrance. Once all nine men were at the door, Larsen peeked in through the mail slot in the door.

"There's no movement that I can see. That doesn't mean there's no one there, just that they might be waiting to take us by surprise. Just be ready for a fight when we breach. Reeves, you've got the lock pick set, go ahead and get us in."

"Now remember, once we breach there is a hallway with two offices on either side and then the door to the factory floor. We need to clear the rooms and then breach that second door. The entrance to the underground bunker is in the north west corner of the building. We will take out any enemy combatants on the floor and make our way to that corner."

"Okay, I've got the door unlocked," said Reeves.

The men entered through the door and met no resistance in the main hallway. They cleared each of the offices and gathered at the entrance to the factory floor. Larsen checked the door, and it was unlocked.

"Alright boys," said Larsen with a huge grin on his face. "The moment of truth. Go! Go! Go!"

He swung the door open, and they were immediately met with gunfire. There were at least ten or more A.I.M. soldiers firing on them from all sides. Everyone quickly found any cover they could and began returning fire.

Dylan was slowly moving from cover to cover, trying to find targets to engage. Within the first minute of the fire fight he had already taken out two A.I.M. agents, causing several more to take notice of him and they concentrated their fire-power on his position. He took cover behind a large piece of machinery and tried to return fire, but any time he tried to take aim, he was met with a hail of bullets. He was pinned down.

"Does anyone have the position of the men firing on me!?" he yelled out.

"Draw their fire and I'll let you know!" replied Reeves.

Dylan grabbed a piece of metal from the ground and stuck it out, drawing fire from the A.I.M. agents.

"Okay, Dylan. There are two men firing on you. Take the one to your ten o'clock. I'll take the other one first to draw the fire of the second one, and then you take him out. Now!"

Reeves took his first shot, and it was a direct hit. The second man turned towards Reeves to return fire, and Dylan broke cover, aimed, and pulled the trigger. Another direct hit.

The shots were steadily becoming less frequent. After what seemed like an eternity, they finally stopped. They had won the battle, but they still had more fighting ahead of them.

"Is anyone down?" asked Larsen.

Amazingly, no one had been hit in the fire fight. Dylan noticed a radio in the hand of a dead A.I.M. agent and picked it up. He pushed the button down and talked into the speaker.

"Hey Kane. It's Dylan. We are about to head down and say "hi." None of your men up here are able to join us because they're all dead. They weren't even able to wound any of us, let alone stop us."

It was silent for several seconds, and then Kane's voice came over the radio. "That's fine Dylan. Those were our worst agents anyways. We won't miss them. There are HOW many of you? Eight? Nine? I've got 20 of our best agents down here waiting to meet you guys. Shane's down here waiting for you to join him too. Isn't that right Shane?"

There was a loud smack, and then Shane cried out in pain.

"You'd better not hurt him asshole! I'm going to really enjoy watching you die. I don't care how many people you have down there with you. I'm going to mow through each and every one to get to you. Shane! Hang in there man we're coming!"

"Can't wait Dylan. Can't wait for you to join us. It will be quite the reunion. When you get down here, Shane and I are waiting at the end of the hall to the left. We also have several kids from the Boys Home down the hallway to the right. You can decide who's more important. Or you can split up and take your chances. But you'd better hurry, I'm getting impatient."

"See you in a minute asshole."

The group made their way towards the back corner of the building to the door of the underground bunker. Dylan punched in the code that Mr. Waters had given him the night he died. The light on the keypad turned green. They were in.

They carefully made their way down the stairs. When they reached the bottom, there were two hallways going in either direction. Larsen stopped and looked down both hallways, and after contemplating for several seconds, he addressed the men.

"Okay, they will most likely have the majority of their men watching the group of kids. Dylan, Reeves, Levitt and Cowden, you four go rescue Shane. The rest of us will go help those kids."

Dylan nodded his head in agreement, and the four men made their way down the hall to rescue Shane and to send Kane, Mooney and Sellers to Hell where they belonged.

18

INTO THE LION'S DEN

Dylan's heart was racing as he, Reeves, Levitt and Cowden made their way down the dark hallway. This was the moment everything had been leading up to. He had been dreaming of revenge since he watched Mooney plunge the knife into Waters' chest. But it wasn't for Waters. Sure, Waters deserved revenge. No one should ever die like that, and he DID help him and Shane escape. But, the revenge he wanted more than anything was for his parents...and Shane's parents. Hell, he wanted revenge for anyone who was ever affected by A.I.M., and he wanted it bad.

They reached the end of the hallway and came to an open door. They took cover on either side of the door, and Reeves peeked around the corner several times to get the layout of the next room.

"Okay, we have a large open room, with six small offices, three on either side with hallways separating each office. I smell a trap, so once we go through this door, expect a fight. Dylan and I will take cover behind the office on the left. Levitt, you and Cowden take the right. We will engage any hostiles and make our way through the room, clearing the offices as we go. Ready, Go!"

As soon as they were through the door, they were met with heavy gunfire. They took cover behind the corners of the first two offices and began returning fire.

"I count six shooters!" Reeves yelled into his earpiece over the sound of the gun fire. "One on the corner of each office. Concentrate fire on the first two corners!"

Just then, Levitt hit the man across the hall from him, and the man went down.

"Got one!" he yelled.

"Guys! There's another hallway running behind the offices!" Cowden yelled. " Levitt and I are going to flank them using the back hallway!"

Cowden and Levitt went to the opposite corner and checked to see if it was clear. Satisfied, they rounded the corner and slowly crept up to the first side hallway; Cowden up front and Levitt behind him to try and take out the shooter. As he came up to the corner, a man came out from behind the second hallway between the offices and unloaded on Cowden and Levitt. Cowden was hit several times and Levitt returned fire, killing the shooter. Then he turned down the first hallway between offices and took out the shooter from behind.

"Cowden is down!" yelled Levitt. "There was a shooter covering the back hallway, but I was able to neutralize him and the one between the first and second office! I'm moving up to flank the next shooter!"

"Dylan, move behind the offices on our side!' yelled Reeves. "Here's a flash bang! Toss it down the hallway and move into position once it goes off!"

Reeves tossed Dylan the grenade. Dylan pulled the pin, tossed it down the hall and waited for it to go off. There was a loud BANG and Dylan rounded the corner and headed to the next hallway and took cover. He moved to the corner of the office along the main hallway and began firing, giving Reeves a chance to move into position.

Levitt came up to the second hallway between the offices and peeked around the corner. There was one agent who was firing his weapon towards Reeves and Dylan, and two more agents on the opposite side of the main hallway. He fired his weapon, hitting the shooter closest to him in the back of the head. The first agent on the opposite side of the main hallway noticed his fellow agent go down and started firing at Levitt, who ducked back behind the office.

"I've got another one! There are two more across the hall, one on either corner. The one nearest me knows I'm here, and he's taken cover behind the door to the office."

"There's a door to the office on this side!" yelled Dylan. "I'll try and sneak up on them. Keep their attention on you!"

Dylan cracked the door to the office open and looked inside. On the opposite corner was one of the shooters, taking cover behind the door and firing at Levitt. Dylan slowly moved into the office. He stayed low and was able to get a few feet from the shooter when the shooter noticed him there, but it was too late. Dylan put a shot directly between the eyes, and the man went down.

Quickly, Dylan went through the door and put two bullets into the other man, who was still watching the back hallway. He didn't even see it coming.

"The two targets are down!" yelled Dylan. "That's six agents down so far! There are still at least two behind the back offices! Levitt and I will start laying down cover fire so you can move up Reeves!"

As Dylan peeked around the corner, he saw who the last two men were. It was Kane and Mooney. Here was his chance for revenge. He began firing towards Mooney who was behind the office on the opposite side of the main hallway, so Reeves could move into position behind him. Once Reeves was in position, Dylan yelled out to the two men.

"Kane! Mooney! It's Dylan! You miss me? All your guys out here are dead. If you give up now and take us to Shane, I MIGHT let you guys live."

It was silent for several seconds, and then Kane's voice boomed out.

"Dylan! Glad you could make it! I think we will take our chances. You might've got some of us, but we aren't letting you through. I've got a detonator here and this whole room is filled with C-4. If you don't give up in the next 5 minutes, we will retreat and blow you and your friends to hell!"

Dylan silently thought about his options. He decided he would go through the office and try to sneak up on Kane and kill him in the same manner as the other agent. He motioned to Levitt and Reeves to engage the two men so he could enact his plan. Reeves and Levitt began to fire on them, and they fired back.

Dylan opened the door to the office and looked around. This office didn't have a second door like the other one did. He wouldn't be able to come up behind Kane now. As he was turning back towards the door he came in, he noticed a small air grate in the back corner of the office. He walked over to it and unscrewed it from the wall. He got down on his stomach and slowly dragged himself through the opening. He was 10 feet behind Kane when he emerged. Crouching down, he made his way up behind him slowly. He took out his knife, stood up, and whispered into Kane's ear.

"Gotcha."

He plunged the knife into Kane's neck. As he was doing this, Mooney saw what was happening, and turned to start firing on Dylan. But Dylan had already grabbed Kane's gun from his hands, and he quickly pulled the trigger twice, hitting Mooney in both kneecaps. Mooney yelled out in pain as he went down. He raised his gun again to try and defend himself, but Dylan pulled the trigger again, this time hitting him in the hand causing the gun to go flying.

As Mooney laid on the ground, writhing in agony, Dylan, Reeves and Levitt walked up to him, Dylan leading the way. When Dylan was standing over him, a look of fear filled Mooney's face.

"I could've killed you right away, but that was too good for you *ROBIN*. I wanted to watch you suffer just a little bit; the way you've made countless kids suffer."

"Go ahead and kill me Dylan, it won't matter. There's no way you are going to be able to save Shane. Sure, we underestimated you, but you most definitely underestimated us. Sellers' is goi..."

Dylan plunged his knife into Mooney's chest, pulled it out and stuck it into his neck. Mooney grimaced in pain, slowly took his last breath, and died.

"Well Dylan," said Reeves. "You got those bastards, and you did it all by yourself. I'm sure there are hundreds, if not thousands of kids who'd love to personally thank you for this. But Shane's down the next hall, and Sellers is with him. We still have another fight ahead of us, so take a minute to bask in this victory, and then we go save Shane and get retribution for your parents."

Dylan shut his eyes and took a nice, long deep breath. *This is it,* he thought. *This is what I've been waiting for. Mom, Dad, I'm not sure if you can hear this, but if you can, this is all for you.*

He opened his eyes, looked at Reeves and Levitt, and opened the door.

19

TAKING A.I.M.

They continued down another long, plain hallway with no rooms attached. The hallway came to an end and broke off to the right. Reeves stopped and looked around the corner.

"Okay, this next area looks like some kind of training area. There are a lot of places to hide behind. It looks like there are two rooms in the back, so that might be where Shane is being held. I didn't see anyone in the open space, but we know they are here somewhere so keep your head on a swivel and your eyes open. We will move through from cover to cover, and if we run into any agents we will engage them and take them out. I'll take point, Dylan you will be in the middle, and Levitt will watch our six. We will assess the situation as needed and make decisions as we go. Got it?"

Dylan and Levitt both nodded. Reeves turned the corner, and they began moving towards the back of the open area where the two rooms were located. They came up to the first barrier, a large brick wall, and took cover behind it. They still hadn't seen anybody.

They moved from behind the wall towards the second

barrier. It was an old car with paint splatters all over it from the training they were doing. They looked in every direction, and there was still no one to be seen.

"I don't like this," said Reeves. "It's too quiet. There should be agents everywhere. This is too easy."

As they were beginning to head towards the next barrier, Levitt yelled out, "Men on our six!"

He began firing on the men behind them, and Reeves and Dylan followed suit as they moved to cover. As Levitt turned to his right to fire on one of the shooters, he was struck in the head from behind and fell to the floor, dead.

"They have us surrounded!" yelled Reeves. "We need to get into better cover! Quick, head to that room over there!"

He motioned to the closest of the two rooms, around 30 feet away. There was no cover between where they were now and the room. They would have to run like hell and hope for the best.

"You go first Dylan! I'll cover you! Keep shooting while you're running. You got this! Go!"

Dylan broke into a sprint towards the room. As he was running, he felt a sharp pain in his side, but kept going. He dove inside the open door, and turned to cover Reeves' escape. But, Reeves was laying on the ground with a hole in his head. Dylan was all alone, wounded, and surrounded by A.I.M. agents.

He crawled behind the nearest desk to take cover. His side was burning like fire now. He lifted his shirt to assess the damage. He had a large, gaping wound in his lower right side. He grabbed a towel that was sitting on the floor and wrapped it around his waist to try and control the bleeding.

All that training for nothing, he thought. *I can't die like this. Not while I'm so close.* The wound in his side was burning like hell, and the makeshift bandage was doing nothing to stop the flow of blood.

The building's loudspeaker chirped on. "We have you surrounded Dylan. Man, you were SO close. I'm here with Shane, and you're only two rooms away. If you give up now, we won't kill you...yet. You still have a chance to live a while longer if you just throw your guns down and give up now." It was Sellers' voice.

"I'd rather die in a hail of bullets than give myself up to you! Kiss my ass Sellers!"

"That's the spirit Dylan! There's that rage I always saw in you! It won't help you anymore, but I love the enthusiasm!"

"I've already killed Kane and Mooney. Why don't you come in here and we can end this right now. Unless you're scared of a wounded teenager. You afraid of me Sellers?!"

He said the words, but he knew they would likely be just that, words. *I'm surrounded, bleeding profusely, and I'll most likely pass out from blood loss soon.* The odds didn't look good, but he had to believe that he still had a chance.

"Come on Dylan. You've got nowhere to go, you're bleeding out, and there's nothing else you can do. We'll be up and running again soon, so you really haven't done anything. I'm going to give you one last chance to throw down those guns and let us take care of that wound, or you can die knowing that nothing's changed."

It was as if Sellers could hear his thoughts, which wouldn't be out of the realm of possibility. Dylan knew things about the world that most people were blissfully unaware of. *You can die knowing that nothing's changed.* Sellers' words hurt. Almost as much as the hole in his side, but not nearly as much as knowing he wasn't able to save Shane. He sat and thought about everything that had happened up to this point. Was this REALLY it? Had he spent all that time and effort to have it all amount to nothing? The thought made him physically ill. Or maybe it was the gunshot wound.

Dylan could tell that time was running out, and he'd soon be dead. He was getting weaker by the second. A sudden rush of panic hit him as he looked down at the pool of blood that was rapidly growing beneath him. *This is it*, he thought. *This is how I die. I'm sorry I couldn't help you Shane.* As Dylan's vision began to dim, the feeling of panic faded, and a sense of calm took its place. *At least I get to see my parents again.* Then everything went black.

20

AWAKENING

B EEP. BEEP. BEEP.
"Hey, go get a nurse. I think he's waking up!"

Dylan slowly opened his eyes, feeling extremely tired and confused. He was in a bright room with white walls and there was a constant, rhythmic beeping sound. Was he dead? Was this Heaven? Where were his parents? He looked over and sitting next to him was Agent Larsen.

"Am I in Heaven?" asked Dylan. "Did you die too?"

Agent Larsen gave him a big smile, chuckled and put his hand on Dylan's shoulder.

"Welcome back Dylan. No, neither of us are dead. You're at UCHealth Memorial Hospital. You were wounded in the fight and passed out from blood loss. We were able to save you though. You'll be perfectly fine. They want to keep you under observation for a week, and then you'll be good to go."

"What happened? Did we win? Were we able to save Shane?"

"They sure did!"

Dylan looked to his right, instantly recognizing the voice. Laying there, in the bed next to his, was Shane. He had gauze wrapped around his head, and his right arm and left leg were wrapped in casts.

"Shane! You're alive! I thought you'd be dead! What happened to you? Are you okay?"

"I'm fine. Sellers hit me a few times, and he broke my arm and my leg while he was interrogating me. But it's nothing, really. I mean you got SHOT! And you nearly died. You're gonna have an awesome scar to impress the ladies with."

"Well," asked Dylan, "what happened? The last thing I remember is Reeves and Levitt being shot and me being surrounded by A.I.M. agents. How am I alive?"

"I'll take it from here Shane," said Larsen. "When we split up, we headed towards the area Sellers said they were holding the kids in. When we got to the room, there were no children anywhere to be seen. Sellers told us that so we would separate, and it worked.

"We were met with gun fire and we were able to hold our own, but we were definitely out gunned. Johnson was shot and was bleeding out. He recognized that we had no way out and made the ultimate sacrifice. He collected any grenades we had, pulled the pins, and made a kamikaze rush towards the main cluster of gunmen, taking two thirds of their men out along with himself. He saved us all with that selfless act."

"After that we had them outgunned and quickly dispatched the rest of them. Then we made our way to help in the effort to save Shane. We came across Cowden's body and heard the gunfight ahead of us and knew you must be in trouble. We followed the sound of gunfire and then it went silent.

"When we got to that last set of rooms, there were several agents surrounding the room you were in. As they were about to open the door, we engaged them and were able to overpower and kill them all. We saw you lying in a pool of your own blood, and we thought you had died. Luckily, Lawsen was a medic in the Marines. We checked your pulse, and you were still with us. He decided to move you back upstairs after he got the bleeding under control. He called an ambulance after taking you outside, and you were brought here. As far as anyone knows, you were just a victim of a mugging gone wrong."

"Remind me to thank him once I see him again," said Dylan. "I owe him my life."

"He'll be by in a few hours, so you can thank him then. So after we got you to safety, the rest of us began the search for Shane. We came around a corner and Sellers was backed into a corner, using Shane as a human shield. He began making his way towards the exit, hoping to get away using Shane as a hostage, but there was no way we could let that happen.

"Snyder tossed a flash bang towards them, and it stunned Sellers just enough for him to let Shane go, and I was able to put a bullet in his head."

"Thank God," said Dylan with a grin. "I was worried he might have gotten away. I would've liked to put the bullet there myself, but as long as he's dead, I'm happy with that. If my parents were here, they'd thank you. I'm so happy they can finally rest in peace."

"What about New Hope and The Denver Toy House?" Dylan continued. "There are more agents out there, and there are kids who need our help still!"

"You didn't let me finish. After we got Sellers, we began our search of the rooms to confirm there were no other agents hiding. We found none. However, we DID find paperwork. Papers identifying every A.I.M. agent from Los Angeles to New York. We have proof of everything. I've already gone through my channels and agents are being arrested as we speak. Any kids they had are all safe. We succeeded in our mission Dylan. YOU succeeded."

Dylan couldn't believe all this was real. He had gone from thinking he was going to die, to finding out that they had succeeded and had saved countless kids from years of torture and having to be mindless killers for an evil organization.

A nurse came into the room holding Dylan's chart, and walked over to Dylan's bed.

"Sir, can you give us a few moments? Now that Mr. Ayers is awake, I need to go over a few things with him."

"Sure, I'll get out of your way. Dylan, Shane, I'll be back a little later. I've got something big to discuss with you two. I'll see you guys in a few hours."

Larsen turned around and left the room, and the nurse closed the door behind him. As she was going over his chart with him, Dylan kept going over what had happened in his head. They had gotten their revenge, but at what cost? He wanted to be happy that it was all over but five men had lost their lives helping him and Shane achieve their goal. After the nurse left, Dylan closed his eyes and fell asleep, thinking about the men who gave their lives so countless others could have theirs back.

EPILOGUE

"So, where do you wanna get lunch today?" asked Dylan.
Shane sat quietly for a few seconds before answering, "Let's go to that Italian restaurant where that pretty waitress works. I've been meaning to ask her for a date."

"Sure, we can go there, but come on man, when do you have time for dating anyone?"

"Oh, I can find some time for her, don't you worry about that."

Dylan and Shane were sitting at their desks in the Denver FBI field office. They had been working for Agent Larsen, who was now the Head of the Counterterrorism Division, for the last four years. They were well respected in the Agency, even at the young age of 23. They had been an integral part in averting several terrorist plots in and around Denver, and they were both awarded the FBI Shield of Bravery for their parts in stopping a plot to kill the Governor of Colorado.

They bought a duplex together after they had been working for the Agency for a year. They had grown so close after all they had been through, and they were just so comfortable together. It was the logical thing to do. Each house was big enough for a family, if they decided to marry in the future. They were family now and always would be.

As they were getting up to go to lunch, Larsen walked up to their desks, and he clearly had something to say. He stopped in front of them, looked back and forth between each of them a few times, and finally spoke.

"You guys aren't going to believe the call I just got. The Los Angeles branch just called me and gave me a heads up."

He paused here for dramatic effect, again looking back and forth between Dylan and Shane with a look of both worry and excitement.

"Well," asked Dylan. "What's up? You're killing us with the dramatics."

"They received a call on their hotline about a group that is recruiting young kids. The caller explained that they were recruiting kids online for what the kids thought was an Acting Agency. He quickly realized it wasn't what he thought when he woke up strapped to a chair with some kind of video playing in front of him. He was able to break free and escape. Now he is in the FBI's custody. Any of this sound familiar?"

"What!?" said Dylan and Shane simultaneously.

"A.I.M. is back?" asked Shane. "How is that possible? We either killed or had every agent arrested, and they are all in prison for life!"

"Are we even sure it's A.I.M.?" asked Dylan. "It could just be a coincidence, right?"

"That's the thing," said Larsen. "This kid identified the head of the organization. The name he gave us is Chase Barnett."

"Chase?!" said Dylan with instant recognition. "I've hated that guy ever since our little altercation at New Hope. He's the Head of A.I.M. now? I always thought he'd turn out to be some sort of criminal, but I never thought he was smart enough to be running an organization like A.I.M.!"

"Well," said Larsen with a grin. "Here's the kicker. Given your history with him and the organization in general, the Los Angeles division wants us to join them out there until the case is solved. They will be putting us up in a house near their office. What do you guys say?"

"When do we leave?" said Dylan.

"I'll go pack my bag now," said Shane.

"Great," said Larsen. "I'll call them back and tell them we will be there within the week."

Dylan and Shane went home that day, excited about their new mission. Neither of them had ever been to California and were excited to experience the Sunshine State.

But there was also a heaviness in the air. A.I.M. was back, and Chase was in charge. Neither of them were totally shocked, but they just figured he'd be a regular criminal, not the head of a newly resurrected criminal organization.

As they packed, they talked about what was to come. How long had he been doing this? How many agents did he have at his disposal? Were they as strong and deep rooted as they had been before?

They packed and talked, eager to take down the organization that had plagued them for so long. The Agency that they THOUGHT they had eradicated four years ago. As they talked, they looked forward to the future and to ridding the country of A.I.M. once and for all.

ACKNOWLEDGMENTS

Thank you first and foremost to my sister, Staci Beuckman, for taking time out of her busy days to be my Editor. I'm glad I could put your Masters in English to work.

Thank you to my two boys, Riley and Zyon. I love you both more than you'll ever know.

Thank you to my mom and dad for having to deal with me as their son for 43 years and counting. I love you.

And last but not least, thank you to all my friends who have been supportive throughout the writing of this book. There are too many to name, but you know who you are.

ABOUT THE AUTHOR

M.A. Williams is an emerging author from Torrance, California, a beach community south of Los Angeles. He is a fan of fiction of all genres, but his favorite is fantasy. He has loved to read his whole life because he loves to get lost in the different worlds each book delivers. He has read hundreds of books, both fiction and non fiction, and he keeps adding to his home library constantly. His favorite authors include, in no particular order, Stephen King, Jonathan Stroud, Chuck Palahniuk, Douglas Adams, Neil Gaiman, Terry Pratchett and Edgar Rice Burroughs. He has two teenage sons, Riley and Zyon. He has several books in the works and is excited to have his work read around the world by ordinary people like him, who love reading as much as he does.

Follow him on his Social Media at:
   Facebook.com/mawilliamsnovels
   Instagram: @M.A._Williams_Novels

To join his mailing list, contact him at:
   mawilliamsnovels@gmail.com

Made in the USA
Columbia, SC
10 November 2021

48558173R00096